I'm being haunted, he said to himself.

It must be that. It can't be anything else.

Haunted.

These things do happen.

I know that now.

I do. He heard Jody speak to him again.

"I shall never leave you. Never."

"Jody."

"Paul . . ."

Also by Jay Bennett:

THE DANGLING WITNESS
THE LONG BLACK COAT
SAY HELLO TO THE HITMAN
THE KILLING TREE
THE BIRTHDAY MURDERER
THE PIGEON
THE EXECUTIONER
SLOWLY, SLOWLY I RAISE THE GUN
I NEVER SAID I LOVED YOU
TO BE A KILLER
THE DEATH TICKET
DEATHMAN, DON'T FOLLOW ME
THE SKELETON MAN*

*Published by Fawcett Books

THE
HAUNTED
ONE

by
Jay Bennett

FAWCETT JUNIPER • NEW YORK

RLI: $\dfrac{\text{VL: 4 \& up}}{\text{IL: 8 \& up}}$

A Fawcett Juniper Book
Published by Ballantine Books
Copyright © 1987 by Jay Bennett

Library of Congress Catalog Card Number: 87-13716

ISBN 0-449-70314-2

This edition published by arrangement with Franklin Watts, Inc.

Manufactured in the United States of America

First Ballantine Books Edition: May 1989

For Moe Steinman
A dear and wonderful man

Chapter

1

The voice came low and clear to him.

"Listen to me," it said.

He held his breath, and then his lips dropped open.

"I am the girl you let die."

"Jody?"

"Jody Miller."

"No," he said.

"Yes. Think it over. You are my murderer. You killed me, didn't you?"

"No. No."

"You did. You let me drown. Out there in the darkening water."

He didn't speak.

"The water covered my lips, my eyes, and then my hair, and I cried out to you for help. But you didn't come."

"I didn't hear you."

"You did. You know you did."

"Please. Please believe me."

"No."

He could almost see her shaking her wet, golden head, shaking it grimly, the water dripping down her face and onto the dry sand.

"You lie," the voice whispered hoarsely. "You didn't come and now I'm dead."

He could see her eyes staring at him, coldly staring at him.

He heard her voice again.

"Dead. But I'm back from the darkening water. Back to torture you."

"No," he said. "This is a trick. Someone's playing a trick on me."

"All life is a trick, you fool."

The voice laughed, harsh and low.

"Stop it," he pleaded.

"I'll never stop it."

"I can't stand it anymore."

"I know."

"You'll drive me to suicide," he said. "I'll kill myself."

"Exactly."

He didn't say anything. His face was white and taut in the shadows.

"Then I will rest. And you will rest. If you can."

The phone went dead.

He stood up slowly and began to moan in a low, agonized tone.

Again and again.

But there was no one in the empty house to hear him.

No one.

In the Beginning

Part One

Chapter

2

In the beginning, everything was fine. Smooth and fine, like shimmering silk in a gentle breeze.

Fine, just fine.

And easy.

Yes, it was like that, he thought bitterly.

In the beginning.

The summer turned out to be a very good one. It was his eighteenth. Full of brightness and soft laughter, with days flowing seamlessly into other sunny days.

Flowing, ever flowing. Endlessly.

Until—the lightning blasted his life into dark fragments.

Sudden, savage lightning, and the sun was gone forever.

It was his first season as a full-time lifeguard. Joe Carson, his chief, assigned him to a fairly deserted stretch of the two-mile-long beach.

"Not much doing here," he said. "A good spot for you to break in."

"Whatever you say, Mister Carson."

"You should know this spot well. You were born in this town. You grew up here, didn't you?"

Paul Barrett nodded.

"You go to Emerson High."

"My last term. I graduate in January."

"What do you want to be?"

"An architect."

"That sounds good."

They were alone on the wide and empty beach. Their shadows were long and dark on the gleaming sand.

"Cordell is a good town," Carson said.

"I like it."

"I've been coming here for thirty-five summers. Been chief for thirty."

Cordell was a summer resort on the south coast of New Jersey. Old and popular with city people for more than a century, the place was crowded and bubbling in the summer months and small and quiet the rest of the year.

Quiet and peaceful.

Paul liked the town both ways.

"Thirty years," Carson murmured, looking away from the youth and out to the morning sea.

A gull flew over them, gray and shining, and then headed out to where the breakers began.

They stood there, two tall figures, stood there watching it set down on the gliding water, firmly and gracefully.

All was quiet and endless about them.

Just as it was at the beginning of time.

"Not much doing here," Carson said. "Even during the hottest part of the day. Very few people use this end. Too far out of the way."

"I know, Mister Carson."

The man turned and looked squarely at Paul.

"Call me Joe from now on."

Paul nodded and felt a glow start within him, warm and pleasurable.

"All my men do, and that's how I want it."

Carson hired on no women. They never came aboard. Not in all his thirty years as chief. The town board looked the other way and left him alone.

He was of the old school. Men have been lifeguards for

centuries. Goes back to the Greeks, to the Aegean Sea.

That's how it was, that's how it is, and that's how it will be.

A long and enduring tradition. Never tamper with tradition. You lose a life, there's no calling it back.

Never.

"Okay, Joe."

I'm part of his team now, Paul thought.

A team that ranks among the best of all the groups all along the East Coast, from Maine to Florida.

Carson's taken me on.

He's just made it official.

"Thanks," Paul said in a low voice.

The man smiled, but it was a wintry smile.

"Now, you know my rules. You know the way I want things done," Carson said.

Paul had spent three weeks at his side, listening and observing.

"Yes."

"Keep within those rules and we'll both be happy."

"I will."

"Good."

The man was silent again, and they stood there listening to the sound of the waves coming slowly in to the shore.

Slowly and lazily, with an eternal, measured motion.

A morning breeze came up and rippled the sand.

Gently. Every so gently.

Some of the gulls took off and cut sharply into the even blue of the pure sky. The others rested on the broad beach.

Immobile, like carved birds of fate, with fixed, dark eyes that glittered in the sunlight.

Carson began to speak again, his voice low and firm.

"From the minute you get up on that life stand to the minute you come down from it at the end of the day, you're a lifeguard. You guard life. Always remember that. Always."

"Yes, Joe."

The man's voice hardened.

"I forgive no one who violates that rule."

"I understand."

The man shook his head grimly.

"'Understand' is not enough. Make it part of yourself. Of your breathing. Of your blood and bones. Keep it before you at all times. Night and day. Never forget that rule. Don't make an enemy out of me. I can be a bad one."

Paul didn't speak.

The man's cold blue eyes bored into the youth, studying him as if meeting him for the first time.

Paul flinched under the steady, penetrating gaze.

And he didn't know why he did that.

Or why a sense of guilt, like a passing black shadow, went over him.

Then he heard the man's voice again.

"Do your job when it has to be done. Quietly and efficiently."

Paul nodded.

"Keep your eyes sharp. Don't trust the water out there. It's full of devil tricks. It loves death. Hates life. Always trying to grab someone by the throat and pull him under and keep him under till there's no breath left in him anymore."

The man paused and breathed out low, his eyes still on the glistening ocean.

"Keep your ears alert. Listen. Always listen. Someone might be calling from out there. Calling for help, calling desperately. I've heard that call, and it goes to your heart and reaches into your soul. I've heard that call, I tell you. And if you don't answer it, you'll be haunted by that cry for the rest of your life. Believe me."

He paused again, his face taut, his body rigid. Finally he turned back to Paul.

"Nothing much happens at this end of the beach. But if it does . . ."

Carson didn't finish the sentence.

"I'll do the job, Joe."

A glint of warmth came into the man's eyes.

"You'd better. Nobody has ever disappointed me. When I choose my men I choose them right."

"You've made no mistake this time."

"I know that."

He put his hand out and Paul shook it. The palm was hard and leathery.

"Start your day," Carson said curtly.

He turned suddenly and walked away, down the long deserted beach, the early morning sun glancing off his gray, short-cropped head and his lean, tanned body.

Paul gazed after him until the figure became a small, shimmering dot.

He turned again to the sea.

The tops of the gliding waves were white and foamy, their centers green and gleaming.

He sighed gently as he looked at them, feeling their soft, eager call to him again and again.

He felt the call in every fiber of his body.

How I've come to love these waters, he said to himself.

Their very sound and sight.

It was here that I learned to swim. First, the breaststroke. Then the crawl. I got better and better at it, season after season, till I was good enough to become an all-state swimming champ.

And now I'm a lifeguard—a member of Joe Carson's famous crew.

On the very same beach I grew up on.

What could be better than that?

"I've got it made," he murmured.

He stood there alone, completely alone, on the vast and sweeping stretch of beach, feeling warm and secure.

So very secure.

"Made."

The word floated away into the enveloping sound of the oncoming waves and was lost there.

Paul Barrett stood silently looking out over the sea a long

while. A tall, loose-muscled figure with clear, fine features and brown hair that now glinted in the morning sun.

His gentle eyes had a hazel tint to them.

He had a tiny scar on his chin, and whenever he was deeply disturbed he would stroke the scar with his long index finger, gently, over and over again.

Now, as he stood there gazing out, he unconsciously stroked the tiny scar. Yet nothing disturbed him. Nothing that he was aware of.

His lone shadow was black and angular on the white sand.

There was nobody around yet.

Nobody.

Finally, Paul stirred and turned away from the hypnotic sea. He slowly climbed up to the top of the glowing life stand and sat down tentatively.

It felt strange to him, being up there alone.

It's mine now, he said to himself.

All mine.

Nobody sits up here but me.

All summer long.

He smiled and adjusted his pith helmet.

Then his sunglasses.

He put some white salve on his nose and cheeks. It was a salve that Joe Carson had concocted years ago and passed out to his men to use.

Paul closed the jar and put it under his large, striped towel. Then he sat back and gazed like a young king, one newly crowned, over his vast and sunswept domain.

The gray gulls still rested on the beach.

Paul felt good.

So very good.

The dark eyes of the gulls glittered.

Chapter

3

Nothing much happened, and as the sunny days went by—it was one of those hot and dry summers—he felt relaxed and happy.

And he did his job well.

Well enough for Joe Carson to smile at him. The eyes that could be like two blue bits of steel were now warm and approving.

"Good work, Paul."

"Thanks, Joe."

"Keep it up, son."

There were the usual routine rescues. Really nothing much there. But once, on a very rough day, he went far out to pull in a drunken fisherman who had fallen out of his boat, and another time he fought a heavy current to rescue a sailor who had never learned to swim but thought that high noon at Cordell beach was the perfect time and place to try.

The sailor came from a small farm in Kansas.

His old mother wrote Paul a letter thanking him for saving her only child's life. It was a fervent and heartwarming letter. Paul kept it folded in his wallet but never showed it to anyone.

Not even to Joe Carson.

He just kept it for himself to read over again at times. The rare times when he felt moody and depressed.

She also sent him a gray wool sweater she had knitted for him. Paul began to wear the sweater toward the end of the season when the early evenings started to turn cold and rainy. It comforted him.

There were the usual cuts and bruises and a few broken bones.

Some lost children and frantic mothers.

And, strangely enough, hysterical fathers.

But all in all it was a very quiet and easygoing life.

A life that he grew to love.

Every glowing morning he could hardly wait to get out of bed, bolt down his breakfast, and then hurry down to the beach toward his sacred spot.

He would sit on the high stand or sometimes down on the hot sand and look out over the sunswept waters of the endless ocean and just think away the soft, flowing hours.

Sometimes in the evening, when the beach was fairly deserted and it was close to the hour of quitting time, he would chat and kid around with some of his school friends who had come by. Once in a while, he would take a few puffs of a joint, just to be sociable with them, first taking a quick, searching look down the slowly darkening beach to see if Joe Carson was anywhere in sight.

He always felt guilty doing that. Not puffing on the joint. There was really nothing to that. He had nothing against smoking grass. It just wasn't part of his life-style. And never would be.

What bothered him was the feeling that in a way he was betraying Joe's trust in him.

That didn't go down too well with Paul.

I shouldn't do it, he said to himself. I just shouldn't.

Yet he did. And it puzzled him.

Until he would forget about it all.

Most of the time he would just stay up there on his shining throne, very much alone, and think.

His sharp eyes scanning the waters.

His ears alert for any unusual sound.

While his mind and imagination played with delight on the bright future.

The last school term, coming up soon, looked like a smooth one, and he was already accepted at Syracuse University with a full athletic scholarship.

Winning the state championship had gotten him a lot of offers.

The scholarship was a handsome one and would go a long way toward paying his tuition and expenses.

He could still keep his summer job on the beach.

All through his years at college, and maybe after that, when he went to Yale's school of architecture.

Why not Yale?

That's the top and I'll get there. I sure will.

And after that?

Who knows?

Quien sabe?

Paul would smile to himself and then think of his two sisters. One married and living in Chicago, settled into being a homemaker and mother.

The other, Jean, a lawyer in San Francisco.

A lawyer not interested in making money but in helping people who needed help.

Somewhat a loner.

In a way like him.

Not too many friends.

She lived with a fellow but wouldn't marry him. Jean always did what she wanted to do. That's why she broke away early and went out to the Coast.

He was offered a scholarship at a college in California near her, and for a long time he thought he'd take it and settle down there. But then he said to himself, I like to be on my own. Just like she does.

He felt very close to Jean. Yet he saw little of her and rarely spoke to her on the phone.

That's the way it is, he shrugged.

And yet I feel closer to her than I do to Dad and Mom.

He lived with his parents in a small wooden house on the outskirts of Cordell. His father was an electrician who did small jobs, and his mother worked as an assistant in the town library.

Never too much money in the house—we've had to do without a lot of things—but all in all we've managed.

Life has been pretty good to me.

And it's going to be better. A lot better.

I'm going to see to it that it is.

Like I have up to now.

And as he sat there thinking this last determined thought —this happened on a clear afternoon—a cloud suddenly passed over the brilliant sun like a giant hand, huge and gray and immutable.

And for some reason, a reason he could not comprehend, Paul felt a sudden fear take hold of him. Cold and chilling and unfathomable.

His eyes became fixed and staring.

His right hand gripped the arm of the stand.

His other hand dangled helplessly at his side.

Then the cloud passed, just as suddenly as it had come, and the sun broke out in an angry splendor, filling the wounded sky with a dazzling and warming brilliance.

The waves eased lazily in to the shore with a low and deep murmur.

The children laughed and played on the bright sand.

Yet Paul still felt chilled.

What's wrong with me? he asked himself.

What?

He took his sweater and draped it over his shoulders. And as he did that, he saw once again the desperate young sailor struggling for breath in the swirling current, crying out for help.

A choking, agonized cry that reached into Paul's very soul.

Chapter

4

It was fate, he said to himself later.

Just that.

And there's nothing you can do about fate.

Nothing.

She came and sat down at the foot of the stand and gazed out to the sea. Sometimes she would knit.

Or sometimes she would read a book.

There was never anybody with her. She always came alone.

She would come in the late afternoon and stay on into the evening, until the setting sun stained the western sky with broad bands of bronze. Then she would slowly gather up her things and turn and walk away from the stand, down the silent beach, Paul's eyes following her until she disappeared from his sight.

And at that instant he would feel deserted and alone, as if he had lost something very precious, never to be found again.

But the next day she would be back, seeking the shade of the stand.

And he would feel restored again.

This happened toward the last days of summer, just before the sun went away and the cloudy and rainy days came in.

At first he did not speak to her. But he would watch her get up, lay the book down on the sand, cover it with her large striped towel, and then go down the beach to the water with a simple, graceful walk.

So pleasant to watch.

And yet there was something about her walk that puzzled and fascinated him, all at once.

It was flat-footed.

Like. . . .

Like. . . .

Ballet dancers.

Like the flat-footed walk of ballet dancers.

That's what it was.

She would walk out into the water until it became deep, and then she would begin to swim with a smooth and powerful overhand stroke.

He saw that she was an excellent swimmer.

She would go far out, far beyond anyone else, and he would see her long, blond hair sparkling in the wide ocean, like shimmering spun gold.

He would watch her, his eyes always scanning the water to see how the other bathers were doing, but ever coming back to that golden head and the flash of white sun on the tanned arms.

She would stay out there almost a full hour.

Then, finally, she would turn and head back.

He would watch her until she came back into the shallows. She would stand and look about her as if seeing the earth for the first time. Then he would see her step out of the water and onto the golden beach.

She would come up toward the stand with that graceful, flat-footed walk of hers, her body so very straight and supple. She would walk slowly and easily, and when she came to the spot where her things lay, she would stop and look about her and take a contented breath of pleasure.

He seemed to feel it, too, in the depths of his being.

He would smile to himself, yet his face was impassive, his eyes hidden behind his dark glasses.

She would stop and pick up her towel and stand there drying herself, all the time shaking her golden head, the long, gleaming hair falling over her bronzed face.

He sat there, watching her.

You're like a goddess, he thought.

A Greek goddess.

You've come out of the sea.

Alone.

When will you go back to the world you've come from? When?

It has to be soon—very soon.

I'll sit here one evening and wait for you and look for you.

I'll feel lost.

So utterly lost.

Yet he never so much as nodded to her, nor did she seem to be aware of him. The two lived in their separate worlds. Until one day, when there were only a few people scattered over the beach.

He had come down off the stand and was leaning against the shadowy side, looking out and watching the sun begin its slow, slow fall into the glowing waters. It was close to seven-thirty in the evening. Suddenly, he found himself talking to her.

She was reading a book. Completely absorbed.

"You're missing something," he said.

The words came out of him before he was aware of them.

She looked up from the book slowly.

"What?"

Her eyes were green. Like the sea, he thought, the sea in the early morning.

"The sun and the sky," he said.

Her eyes were cool as she looked at him. Steady and cool.

17

"What about them?"

Her voice was soft and low. It was the first time he had ever heard it. And he said to himself, It's just the voice I imagined she had. It matches her so very well.

"They're beautiful to see. Especially at this time of the day," he said.

"I've seen it before."

"It's always good to see it again. I never get tired of it."

"You don't?"

He shook his head.

"Never."

He took off his dark glasses and held them in his hand.

"But you see a sunset every day," she said.

"It's different every day."

"If you want it to be."

"Maybe."

She smiled and looked away from him and out to the horizon. There was a freighter far out on the water, black and heavy looking, but its bow was burnished by the dying rays of the sun.

They both watched the boat move slowly, ever so slowly, black smoke wisping up, until finally the boat dipped away, falling over the rim of the horizon, and was gone from their sight.

She sighed gently.

"Yes, it was beautiful," she said.

"It is," he murmured, looking down at her.

She was his age, he thought, and yet she had such poise, such smooth self-assurance.

Then he said to himself, All beautiful girls have that.

And then he said, No, they do not.

"Not all of them," he said aloud.

She looked up questioningly at him.

"What?"

"It's—it's nothing."

"Oh."

Her eyes were studying him.

18

He put his glasses back on.

"You would've missed it," he said.

"The sunset?"

"Yes."

She was silent.

"Thought I'd point it out to you."

"You did. Thanks."

There was a gently mocking smile in the green eyes.

"I'm Paul. Paul Barrett," he said.

"Jody."

"Just Jody?"

"Jody Miller."

"I like the name."

"Why?"

"Oh, I don't know. But I like it."

"I see."

"You come from around here?"

She shook her head and her hair sparkled with reddish glints.

"The city."

"New York?"

"Is there any other city but New York?"

"I guess not."

She laughed softly.

"You come from there?" he asked.

She shook her head.

"No."

And she never did tell him where she came from.

He only found out later.

"You're staying here a while?"

"A while."

"And then you'll be going back to the city?"

"That's what I'm planning to do."

"When is that going to be?"

"Oh, a week or so."

"I see."

"Do you?"

There was an amused sparkle in her eyes. And he thought to himself, She looks on me as a kid. She goes out with older men.

She's just playing with me.

I should've kept my mouth shut.

"What are you reading?" he heard himself say.

She held up the book.

"*History of the Ballet*," he read aloud.

"That's what it is," she said gently.

"You dance?"

"Uh-huh," she nodded.

"I'll bet you're very good at it."

"Why do you say that?"

He shrugged. "Just feel it."

"Just by looking at me?"

He hesitated. "Well, I. . . ."

Her eyes were directly on him. "Just that? Feelings?"

She's playing with me, he thought desperately. "I—I guess so."

She suddenly smiled, and it was a gentle smile.

"I'm fair," she said in her low voice. "Some people think I might get better."

"People who know their stuff?" he asked.

"Perhaps."

"You must love ballet."

She nodded. "I do. Or I wouldn't be in it. It's very hard work."

"I know."

She looked at him. "You do? How?"

He adjusted his glasses.

The way she was looking at him now made him more unsure of himself. And he thought, What's the matter with me? I'm always okay with girls. I'm easy with them and they're easy with me.

He began to speak again.

"Anything you want to do well demands work," he said. "Work and dedication."

20

I'm beginning to sound like my swimming coach, he thought hopelessly.

"True," she murmured.

She's laughing at me, he thought. But he couldn't help himself and went on.

"It *is* true. I've put hundreds of hours into my swimming. I still have to practice every day. I go out every morning before people come onto the beach. Just go out and swim and swim. All kinds of weather."

"You must be very good," she said.

"I'm a champ."

The instant he said that, he felt like a fool. A kid showing off his medals.

He wanted to turn and climb up the stand and sit down and gaze out at the sea and forget that he ever saw her. Or ever spoke to her.

But he stood there. Held to the spot.

"It's good to be a champ," she said.

He flushed and quickly changed the subject to ballet.

"I've gone into the city and seen some fine ballets there. At Lincoln Center."

"It's hard to believe that," she said.

"Why?"

"Because most people our age don't care very much about ballet. They don't even know it exists," she sighed.

His voice hardened just a bit. "I'm not like most people," he said.

She smiled. "I guess you're not."

"I've watched many ballets on public television over the years. Seen a lot of them."

"I'm sorry. I believe you," she said gently. "I shouldn't have said what I just...." Her voice trailed off into the silence.

"That's okay," he said.

"I shouldn't have," she murmured.

She looked away from him and out to the darkening horizon, a shadow settling over her face.

He listened to the dull, measured sound of the waves and then looked at her clear profile, so sharply etched against the shimmering twilight, and a fear crept into his heart, as if he knew, deep inside his being, what would happen to him. What would happen to him. And to her.

His hands trembled just a bit.

And then he heard her voice coming through the sound of the waves, coming to him as from a distance.

"*Giselle*?" she asked.

"What?"

She had turned toward him now.

"The ballet. You must have seen it."

"Oh. Yes, I have," he said.

"Do you like it?"

"Up to a point. Then I think it tails off and I lose interest."

Her eyes coolly studied him.

"I don't agree with you," she said.

He shrugged.

"That's what makes horse races," he said.

"Horse races and ballets," she laughed.

"That's a combination," he laughed.

And then they were silent a moment.

The peaceful quiet of the murmuring ocean lay about them, and then she began to speak again.

"I may dance in it," she said. "In the fall."

"You will?"

"I don't know for sure. I've already danced in *Giselle*. A minor role."

"When?" he asked.

"Last season. With a small ballet company in Chicago."

"I wish I'd seen you," he said.

She shook her head. "I wasn't very good in it."

"I'm sure you were."

The lengthening shadows moved over her face. Her green eyes glowed softly.

You're so beautiful, he thought. So very beautiful.

Then he heard her voice.

"How did you get interested in ballet?"

"What?"

"How did it happen?" she asked.

"Oh. My sister took me to it when I was a kid. She's the one who got me very interested in all the arts," he said.

"All?"

He laughed softly. "Some of them."

"She sounds like a beautiful person."

"She is," he said.

"You still go to the ballet with her?"

He shook his head and a wistful look came into his eyes. But she did not see the look, for he still wore his dark glasses.

"Do you?" she asked again.

"No. She's out on the West Coast now. Lives there."

"Then you don't go anymore?" she asked.

"Sometimes. But not as much."

"Oh." She seemed to be disappointed.

"I go with some girlfriends when I do," he said.

"You have girlfriends?"

"Why not?" he said.

"Why not?" she echoed.

She smiled, and he could see that she was gently playing with him.

"Many?"

"A few," he admitted.

"Just enough."

"Right."

A soft breeze came up and made her hair stray. He watched her put her hand to her head and stroke the wandering strands back into place with a graceful, simple motion.

He had sometimes watched his mother do that with the same graceful gesture.

And he remembered how his mother had once been a beautiful woman and then almost overnight lost it all.

One gray winter morning he looked at her, and she was

23

having an argument with his sister Jean, and the beauty was gone. Vanished. Never to return.

He remembered feeling a great pity for his mother. And a heartbreaking anger.

One should hold on to one's beauty—tight—and not go about and destroy it before its time.

That is what she had done.

Paul kept looking at Jody and then out to the water.

They didn't speak for a while.

A shadowy silver jet suddenly flew over them and headed out over the sea. They watched it until it disappeared into the oncoming darkness, the lights winking out.

"It's late," she said.

He didn't speak.

"I'd better be going."

She turned away from him and started to put her things together.

"Can I help you?" he offered.

She shook her head. "I can do it."

But he knelt at her side and silently helped her. When they were done, they both stood up, almost at once. Close to each other.

He felt a tightening in his chest.

"You should take off your dark glasses when you talk to a girl," she said.

He stared at her.

"Why?"

"Because you have beautiful eyes," she said.

Then she turned and walked away from him.

Chapter

5

He was sitting on the stand in the darkness, looking out to the sea, his eyes watching the running lights of an anchored fishing boat, when he heard the curt voice below him.

"Paul?"

"Yes?"

"What are you doing up there?"

It was Joe Carson.

"Oh. Just sitting here."

"Anything wrong?"

"No."

"Then come on down and let's get going."

Paul came down slowly from the shadowed stand and then stood beside the silent man.

Carson glanced sharply at him.

"Been waiting for you to come in and check out. I thought something had gone bad up here."

"I'm sorry, Joe. I didn't realize it was so late."

"You've never done this before."

"I know."

"Well?" asked the man.

"It's nothing. Just forgot myself."

He started to walk at Carson's side. Ahead of them they

25

could see the glow of lights from the amusement area. It was to the right of them and just off the border of the long, curving beachfront.

"Is it something at home?"

"No."

"Everything all right there?" asked Carson.

"Sure, Joe."

"Something's troubling you," the man said.

"I'm okay," said Paul.

"You never did this before," Carson muttered.

"I know."

And Paul wanted to say to him, I really don't know why I kept sitting up there after the sun went down.

And Jody gone away from me.

Sitting there alone in the darkness, nobody else left on the beach, not even the ever-silent gulls, just sitting and listening to the heavy sound of the waves coming in again and again, without letup.

I really don't know.

I was looking at those night waves and thinking about her and about life. And for some strange reason, about death.

Yes, death.

I saw once again the young sailor struggling for his last gasp of breath in that cruel current. Struggling there, and the green water like two dark hands clutching at his throat, trying to take him down under for good.

And then I got to him.

I beat death that time.

Yes, I did.

Joe, I was thinking of that.

And of how beautiful she is.

So alive and breathtaking.

Yes, Joe, she does take my breath away.

Like nobody else ever did before.

I was thinking of all that, Joe.

"I'm sorry," Paul said.

"No sweat. Just don't do it again."

"I won't."

"Be sure you don't." This time the man's voice was harsh.

Paul flinched.

The two continued their way along the empty beach, not saying anything to each other for a while.

The night was warm, the air was still.

A rocket suddenly sped up into the dark sky over them and then burst into a shower of glowing sprays, lighting up the sky with a cold brilliance. Then all was dark again, as before.

Another rocket soon followed. Then three more went up in quick succession and burst into a great cluster of sparkling stars.

"Show's a bit early tonight," Paul murmured.

Carson shook his head.

"On time. It's later than you think."

The two walked on, their bare feet kicking up little spurts of dark sand, and Carson began to speak again.

"Paul."

"Yes, Joe."

"Listen to what I have to say to you."

The man paused and Paul waited.

"I know I'm a hard man to get close to," Carson said in a low and even voice. "That's the way I am. But if you ever have something you want to talk over with me—you know what I mean."

Paul nodded silently.

He could see the hard profile of the man against the sky's intermittent glow, the shape of the close-cropped head and the line of the thin, tight lips.

He remembered that Carson had been an infantry captain in the Korean War. Won some medals, and then one day, after visiting a friend in the Vet's Hospital, he walked out of the building and threw the medals away on the grass.

The two were silent, and then Paul heard Carson's voice again.

"I never had a son, Paul. That's the way it worked out with me. Never had one."

"Ever marry, Joe?"

"Yes."

"And?"

"She died young."

"Oh," Paul said softly.

"A good part of me went with her. The better part."

As they came closer to the amusement area he could see Joe Carson's face much better. And the concerned eyes.

"So remember what I said to you," said Carson.

"I will," he nodded.

"Check in and go on home, Paul."

Then he watched Carson walk away from him and merge into the darkness of the night.

Paul stood there, listening to the waves pound the shore with an increasing intensity.

And with each breaking wave he heard Carson's toneless voice.

She died young.

Young.

Paul turned away from the dinning sound of the ocean and hurried into the locker room. He dressed quickly and then got out of there.

Away from the sound and sight of the water.

Chapter
6

He didn't feel like going home, so he ate his supper at one of the pizza stands and then wandered around the amusement area.

There was a great restlessness in him—he didn't know where it came from—a restlessness and a dark sense of foreboding.

He felt as if he had been swimming far out in the sunswept ocean, full of the sweep and joy of life, and suddenly, almost insensibly, had found himself drawn into a powerful and mean current, a current that was taking him farther and farther away from the safe and shining shore.

And he didn't know how to get out of the current, how to break free of it.

There was something so inevitable about it all.

So desperately inevitable.

Like fate.

He stopped to talk to Ralph Nelson who worked at the Carvel stand. Ralph was in his class at school.

"We're going over to Cliffside at nine. How about coming along?"

Paul hesitated.

He liked Ralph and liked being with him.

"I don't know what I'll be doing tonight. Maybe I'll go on home."

Ralph shook his head and turned away to ring up a sale.

"Last days of the season coming up. Take advantage of it, Paul."

"Not in the mood."

"Soon be back in school and all that jazz. The grind again."

"I know," said Paul.

"Joan and Ellie are coming along," Ralph said temptingly.

Paul had gone out with Joan and it had worked out fine. He stood there hesitating.

"Come on, Paul," urged Ralph as he stepped back to the register.

"Okay," Paul said. "Count me in."

"Make it nine."

"I'll be there."

"The back parking lot," said Ralph.

"Sure thing."

He waved to Ralph and started to move on.

"Joan's car," said Ralph.

"Okay," said Paul.

He felt a little better. Joan's good company, he thought to himself. We get along swell with each other. So it looks like a good night coming up. I could use one like that.

He walked around the noisy, bustling amusement area aimlessly, just killing time. He stopped to talk to some people he knew from the beach and then walked on, past the Cyclone, past the parachute jump, past the Ferris wheel. Suddenly he stopped stock-still and looked back to the wheel again.

And he saw her.

She was sitting on one of the open, swinging seats, high off the ground.

"Jody," he whispered.

He felt a catch in his breath as he stood there watching

30

her go up, up, over the lighted arc and then come slowly down again.

The wheel paused to take on some more passengers and she was stranded there, poised against the blue-dark sky, looking straight ahead of her.

Out to where the dark sea was.

And it seemed to him that her eyes were sad and poignant.

Almost lost.

As if she yearned to be back in the warm, sunlit water again. Not stranded in the glittering, cold, and hostile sky.

He kept looking up at her, and he was sure that she hadn't seen him yet.

He waited, and it seemed to him an interminable length of time before the lighted wheel brought her down and she stepped off and onto his earth again.

He went slowly over to her.

"Jody?"

She turned and looked up at him. "Paul?"

And that's all she said, but there was a smile in her large, gentle eyes. And it made him feel warm inside.

She wore a white silk blouse with light gray summer slacks, her golden hair was drawn back into a bun, and he said to himself, I can see now that she's older than me, she must be.

She's in her twenties, I'm sure of it.

This is hopeless. I'm just a green kid to her.

"You want to have some coffee, Paul?" she asked.

"What?"

"If you have the time."

"Time?"

"And would like to have some coffee with me," she added.

He suddenly grinned.

"Sure, Jody."

"You know of any good places?"

"Good?"

"Where the coffee is decent. I've had some bad luck lately," she said.

He laughed softly.

"Sure."

"Then let's go," she said.

He started to walk at her side, and as he did, he forgot about Cliffside and about Joan and Ralph.

Completely forgot about them.

He had entered a new and magical world.

I think she likes me, he said to himself.

He walked tall next to her, tall and straight and proud, hoping someone he knew would see him then.

Yes, I think she does.

Then she gently linked her arm in his, and he knew for certain that she did.

Chapter

7

They sat high on his life stand, the two of them, and looked out over the dark sea. The glow from the amusement park had disappeared into darkness, the time was very late, and only the night sky with a spread of fading stars was above them.

They had been silent for a while.

A glow was within him, warming his entire being.

I've never felt this way in all my life, he said to himself. Just having her here at my side, and we two alone in all the world.

Nothing around us but the beach, the sea, and the wide, wide sky.

We're back to the beginning of time.

Just Jody.

And me.

Nothing else seems to exist.

Or matter.

Nothing.

Later on, when he looked back on it, he found that he had done most of the talking. And it was all about himself. She wanted to know everything about him. As if she felt that she would never see him again. And this was her only chance to truly know him.

She said very little about herself.

A few scattered words that added up to nothing.

Nothing.

She could just as well have come out of the sea for all he managed to find out about her.

But she did speak about ballet.

"Ballet is all that matters to me, Paul. I think of nothing else."

"It's your life," he said.

"It is. Ever since I was a child."

"Since then?"

She nodded.

"Without ballet I would surely die," she said.

Then she said something he never forgot.

"One of the greats in ballet has taken me on as his personal project. He's like a Balanchine. And he has high hopes for me."

She paused and then went on. In the background he could hear the sound of the waves.

"Believes I'll be one of the best. Says dancers like me come only once in a lifetime. I don't really believe that. But it's nice to hear those words."

Her wave-green eyes lighted up.

"I do have great hopes. I really shouldn't," she said.

He leaned forward to her.

"You should. You'll make it, Jody."

"How do you know?" she asked.

"How?"

"Yes."

"I just do, Jody," he said.

She laughed quietly.

"You're just being nice to me."

He shook his head fiercely.

"I tell you I know it."

And she was silent. And then she said, "You're a champ.

34

You know what it means to win it all, don't you?"

"Yes," he said.

"It must be a great feeling."

"It is," said Paul.

Then, for some reason he couldn't fathom, her eyes darkened and she looked away from him to the white foamy line of the breakers, white against the lingering darkness.

"Sometimes I think it's all words, just words," she said in a low voice. "Like that streak of foam out there. Blows away and nothing is left. I'll never make it, Paul. Never. Something terrible is going to happen to me."

A shock of fear went through him.

"You mustn't think that way, Jody," he said.

She shook her head sadly, still not looking at him.

"But I do. I do."

Her voice almost broke.

It was then that he put his arms around her.

Chapter

8

He never found out where she lived.

When it came down to it, he realized that he knew nothing about her personal life.

But one thing he did know: He was desperately in love with her. She was ever in his heart and mind.

When he kissed her, he knew that she loved him, too.

He could've sworn his soul on that.

"I've never met anybody like you before, Jody," he whispered.

"Never?" There was a playful, teasing look in the sea green eyes.

"No."

"I don't believe you," she said.

"Why don't you?"

"Because, Paul, you're very attractive. You know that."

He shook his head. "I don't know."

"You're modest."

"Let's drop it," he said.

"You're blushing."

"It's dark. How can you tell?"

"I can sense it." She laughed softly.

"Jody," he breathed.

And he kissed her again.

Then they were silent. The last of the day's darkness gathered about them as they strolled toward her motel. He could no longer see her green eyes.

Only soft darkness.

It was close to morning when he left her.

"I'll see you tomorrow on the beach," she said.

He smiled. "You mean today. It's already today."

"Yes. So it is."

"What time will you be there, Jody?"

"About four."

"Couldn't you make it earlier?" he asked.

"Why?"

"Because I miss you already."

"You do?" she said teasingly.

"You know I do."

She laughed softly and nodded. "I do."

The sunlight was already gleaming on her hair. Soft, stray gleamings.

"Then it'll be earlier, Jody?"

"I'll try," she said.

"Please."

She nodded and her golden hair flashed.

"All right. Earlier," she promised.

"Thanks, Jody."

He kissed her and turned to go.

"Oh, Paul."

"Yes?" He stood hesitantly on the threshold.

"Don't wear your dark glasses."

"Why not?" he asked.

"Because I like to look at your hazel eyes."

"Oh, cut it, will you, Jody?" But his voice was soft to her.

"Why?"

"Because I don't like it."

"Can't you take a compliment?" she asked.

"It's not a compliment to me."

"Even if I tell you you're tall and bronzed like a Greek god?"

And before he could say anything, she laughed brightly and closed the door of the motel room.

All the way home, he thought of her. Only of her. Coming out of the seawater and onto the white beach, the sun shining on her golden hair.

"Jody," he whispered. "You are the Greek goddess. You. Always you."

Then, once again, he heard her gentle, joyful cry as she saw him coming down the beach to greet her.

Chapter

9

But he never did see her again.

Never. That is, he never saw her again, alive.

There was a message for him at the motel.

I've been called back to the city for some special re-hearsals. I'll try to see you toward the end of the week. It's more likely that I'll be able to swing free sometime next week.

Till then, Hazel Eyes,
Jody

Don't wear those black glasses. They scare me.

He took the letter and slowly and carefully folded it and then, later, he slowly and carefully put it away in his desk drawer. To read and look at again and again.

Once he came into his room, and there was his mother reading the letter, tears in her eyes, and he grabbed the letter from her hands and shouted at her.

But that was later on.

Now he found that each day, each hour, waiting for Jody to return, was a torture. He could no longer sit quietly on the stand for any length of time, but had to come down onto the dry, hot sand and restlessly patrol the beach.

Sometimes he would look out over the shining water and see her swimming far, far out, and his breath would stop, and he would swear to himself that it was Jody swimming far, far out, the golden hair and the flashing arms—and then he would turn away desolately.

She's never coming back, he said to himself.

The sunny days became cold. Clouds lowered in the sky.

As if she had taken the bright sun away with her.

It began to rain. Chilling, heartless rain.

And he said to himself, If I only knew where to call her. Just to hear her voice.

Just that.

I'd be satisfied.

I would.

Dear God, I tell you I would.

And then he wondered, Why doesn't she call me? She knows where to call. I told her where I live.

She knows and yet she never calls.

It made him bitter to think of that.

Ballet is her life, she said that to me. Her life, and she's now caught up in it and I'm not part of it.

Simple as that.

Simple and cruel as that.

I'll never see her again.

Never.

As the days went by, fewer and fewer bathers came to his part of the beach. The season was coming to a dreary end. And he thought to himself wearily, How bright it was when it all started how full of sunshine and quiet joy.

Now it was all turning into ashes.

There were times when he was practically alone on the beach. Especially in the last hours of the gray days. Then the time lay heavily on him, and it became an almost unbearable weight. He just didn't know how to get through those torturing hours. Finally, in desperation, he got hold of some joints, and each evening he would sit on the beach, lean back against the stand, and take some puffs.

Just enough to deaden the pain of the long and hopeless waiting for her.

One evening when he went in to check out, he found Joe Carson looking sharply at him.

"Everything all right up your way, Paul?"

"Yes, Joe. It's a deserted beach these days."

"I know."

"Nobody around me for hours."

"There's something around your eyes that I don't like," Carson said.

Paul flushed.

"What do you mean?"

Carson turned curtly away from him.

"Nothing. Go on home."

And Paul said to himself, That's the last time I do it.

But it wasn't.

Chapter
10

The very last day of the season.

That's when it happened.

During the last hour.

Almost to the last minute.

As if fate had sardonically worked it out to the very end.

He was sitting on the sand, his back against one of the posts of the lifeguard stand, staring dully ahead of him.

It had rained most of the day, a chill drizzle. Now the sun had come out, a faint evening sun, its last thin rays spread out over a soft and undulating ocean.

There was nobody else on the beach with him. Only some silent, gray gulls.

The end is coming, he said to himself. The end of the season. A few more long, long minutes and it will all be over.

He lit a joint and drew in the smoke. This time his mind clouded over and the beach and the reach of water seemed to move farther away from him. He sat as if in a little cell of his own. Yet his pain broke through its walls, sharp and unyielding.

He shook his head.

What will I do? he thought bitterly.

How will I stop thinking of her?

Dear God, how?

He closed his eyes a while, and then something strange stirred within him and he found himself slowly rising to his feet.

"Jody," he whispered.

His eyes grew large and he stared out over the glistening, ruddy water, and he thought he could see her far out, her hair glowing. She was waving to him to come to her, waving joyously.

He felt a warm and dizzying thrill run through his entire being.

"Jody," he said again.

His voice sounded strange and far-off to him, as if it came from another being.

He took a few steps forward, and then his mind clouded up again and his vision wavered.

He stopped and almost swayed.

"It's nothing. Nothing," he mumbled.

Then he flung his hand angrily at the deceiving ocean and slowly sat down again.

He stared dully, unseeingly ahead of him.

One of the gulls abruptly took off and flew low over the water, catching the rays of the dying sun, but he was unaware of it.

He puffed again and then sat back. But now there was no sharp, piercing bitterness when he thought of her, only sad and hopeless resignation.

She would never come back.

She lied to me, he thought.

Why not?

It was all a game to her.

I was just someone to pass the hours with.

And all the time, in the back of his mind, he thought he could hear Jody's voice trying to break through the walls of his cell, calling desperately to him.

It's all a lie, he said to himself.

43

Life itself is a lie.

So what?

What's new for breakfast this morning, Mom?

Old ham and eggs.

"Hazel Eyes," he muttered aloud and laughed hoarsely.

And then he laughed again.

"Don't wear black glasses. It scares me." That's what she had said.

He fumbled in the sand for his dark glasses. He would wear them. He would. His hand scooped along, feeling the wet grains between his long fingers, and it was at that instant that he felt the agonized, heartwrenching cry break through and into him.

"Paul!"

It seemed to reach up and sound against the walls of the sky.

Reverberating.

Then he heard it again.

"Paul!"

It came over the water to him, and now he was on his feet, and this time his senses were washed clean and he saw her, yes, this time he saw her, her hands thrust out desperately to him. Then the cry broke from him.

"Jody!" he cried. "Jody!"

It came from the very depths of his torn being.

Chapter
11

He never felt the water, never was aware of how desperately he was swimming out to her, with all his skill and strength and power. It was the fastest he had ever swum in all his life.

But this time he lost.

He came to the still-swirling water, the very spot, and then, without getting breath, he dived and went deep, deep, until his head was bursting and his ears pounding, the blood trickling from his nostrils, and then he saw her and got his arms around her, tightly, oh, ever so tightly, and he went up, up, and broke through the placid surface of the water.

Then he swam fiercely, savagely to the saving shore, clutching her tightly in his hold.

You'll live, Jody.

You'll live, he said over and over with each iron stroke. But deep inside himself he had started to weep.

Chapter

12

A cluster of silent lifeguards stood around her. The evening shadows dulled the luster of her wet, golden hair. Her large green eyes were open and still filled with the terror of the clutching water.

Paul sat against the stand and stared vacantly at the sea.

Joe Carson came over and sat down by him.

"She's gone," Joe said.

"Yes."

And Paul wondered at how calm his own voice was, calm and dead. Inside there was no feeling, no deep emotion. Nothing.

"Ed said she started swimming from his beach. She first asked him if you were on duty today," said Carson.

Paul didn't say anything.

"She wanted to surprise you. That's what she said to him."

"Yes," Paul said.

"She was doing fine and then something happened out there. A cramp, I'd say," Carson said quietly.

"Something happened."

This time there was a quiver in Paul's voice.

Carson put his hand on Paul's shoulder.

"You did your best. Your very best. Ed says you were

magnificent. You gave it your all," said the man.

Paul's hands clenched and then slowly unclenched.

"You just got to her too late. She was too far out."

Paul didn't say anything.

"You went out just as soon as you saw she was in trouble."

I didn't, Paul said to himself.

I went out when it was already too late.

Much too late.

I could've saved her.

I know that now.

She must've been calling for help and I sat back.

Just sat back and took another puff.

All the time she was drowning.

All the time.

Why am I so dead inside of me?

Why don't I break down and cry?

Why?

Dear God, why?

He heard Carson's soft voice come through to him.

"Go on home, Paul. We'll take care of things."

"I'll stay," Paul said.

"There's nothing more for you to do."

"I'll stay."

Carson sighed low.

"Sure. Whatever you want, son."

The man put his hand on Paul's head, touched the hair gently, and then got to his feet.

Paul saw Carson start slowly back to the cluster and then suddenly pause and look down at the sand.

He stooped and picked up a crumpled cigarette.

He put it to his nose and then crushed it in his large fist and threw it away from him.

He stood there motionless.

Then he turned to look at Paul.

Their eyes met.

The man's face was hard as stone.

The Haunting

Part Two

Chapter
13

He remembered reading in Oscar Wilde's poem, *The Ballad of Reading Gaol*, the bitter line, "Yet each man kills the thing he loves."

And he said quietly to himself, He does, he does.

It was strange to him that he was able to go about his life as he had done in the past. The school term started and he went to his classes and sat in the rooms and did his studies very well and talked to his schoolmates and went out with them, but something within him had died.

Everybody said he had become quiet.

Quieter than before.

Almost pensive.

That's the way one of his favorite teachers spoke of him.

Pensive, she said. An inner sadness. As if something very poignant had happened to him during the summer. And when she questioned him very delicately, he said nothing had happened.

Nothing.

And she drew back and let him alone.

That's the way he wanted it.

He knew that he didn't care anymore what happened to him. All the plans and the dreams had crumbled.

I'm going through the motions, he said to himself.

That's it.

As if I had been programmed from before.

It's in the computer and it's going to stay there.

Strange, I don't even think of Jody as much as I used to. There are times, hours, long hours, when I don't even remember her.

Isn't it strange?

As if I had never even met her, never saw her come out of the sea and walk up the beach to me.

Joy in her green eyes.

Those soft, green eyes.

Now they are closed shut.

The joy gone out of them.

They came here and took her away and buried her in some small cemetery in some small Midwestern town and that's the end of her.

And of me.

How well I know that.

Joe Carson didn't even say a word to me again. Not a word. Just went down south to the Florida beaches and that's it.

Wrote me off as a disgrace to the profession and a traitor to his friendship.

Convicted me without a trial.

Never even heard my side of it.

And what is your side, fool?

You tell me.

You let her die, didn't you?

You're silent.

You've nothing to say.

Verdict is handed down and you're convicted.

That's that.

The phone rang and it was his sister calling from San Francisco. Outside the window, darkness had already fallen.

A silent darkness.

He didn't turn on the light, just sat there, the phone in his hand, listening to her talk.

"Mom says you've become very quiet."

"I've always been quiet," he said.

"You don't talk much."

"So what's new out your way, Jean?"

But she persisted.

"Are you in love?"

"What?"

"Or is it none of my business?"

"I'm not in love," he said.

"What is it then?"

"Let it alone, Jean," he said grimly.

There was a pause on the other end. He kept looking out the window at the dark night.

Then he heard her say, "You want to come out here for a little while?"

"What for?"

"Oh, just to see each other and talk. We always got along very well with each other."

"We did," he said.

"Well?"

Jean, live your life and I'll try to live mine.

Whatever is left of it.

"I can't get away," he said. "I've got exams coming up."

"Paul."

"That's what it is."

"They'll give you makeup exams later on," she said.

"They won't."

"Come on, you've got an excellent school record," she persisted.

"How do you know?"

"You always have," she said.

"So?"

"So come out for a little while, Paul."

"I'll stay here, Jean," he said.

"No changing your mind?"

"No," he said with finality.

There was disappointment in her voice when she spoke again, disappointment and defeat.

"Thought you'd come out," she said.

He knew he was hurting her.

"I'm not."

"No way I can persuade you?"

"No way, Jean."

"You know how much I love you, Paul."

"Yes."

"And I know how much you love me. I do know it."

He was silent.

"Well?" she asked.

"No."

"I'm concerned about you, Paul."

"Why?"

"Mom is worried."

"Mom is always worried," he said coldly.

There was a pause on the other end.

He could almost see his sister's drawn face and the anxious look in her eyes as she sat holding the phone so many, many miles away from him.

He wanted to reach out and touch her.

To comfort her.

And then he thought of Oscar Wilde's words, *We kill the things we love*, and he said to himself, She is one I love and I am hurting her so terribly.

So very much.

Tonight she won't sleep.

I know it.

How well I know it.

And yet there is nothing I can do about it. Absolutely nothing.

Paul heard his sister's voice again.

"I want you to promise me one thing," she said.

"Yes?"

"If you really need me, you'll call."

"I won't really need you," he said.

"Promise."

"I tell you I won't."

Her voice became hard.

"Promise," she said fiercely.

He sat back in his chair and didn't speak.

"Paul, I want you to promise," she repeated.

"All right," he finally said.

He heard her sigh.

"Take care of yourself."

"I will."

Then he heard the click and put down the phone.

He sat there a long while, and then he got up and went to the mirror on the wall and looked into it.

His face was white and drawn.

There was a look in his eyes that almost frightened him.

Chapter
14

The sun came out with a fierce and savage brilliance. The days became intensely hot, and it could just as well have been summer again.

As if it were starting all over, he said to himself.

As if there had never been a summer this year.

And this was the true beginning.

The other was false and a cruel illusion.

It was Saturday morning, the air was bright and dry, the sky a brilliant blue, and the clouds large, soft, and a shining white.

He stared up at them, something stirred alive within him, and for the first time in weeks he felt himself drawn to the beach, with an almost irresistible hunger.

He felt a driving, urgent need just to feel his bare feet on the hot sand and see once again the glistening green waves break with white foam.

To feel the ocean breeze play over his face and body. Gently. Ever so gently.

The way it did when he sat high on the lifeguard stand and gazed out over his wide and serene domain.

And dreamed his golden dreams.

He felt himself tremble as he came closer and closer, and

his breath came short as he saw the beach as if for the first time.

Then he stopped abruptly and his lips shut in a tight line. For he heard the sound of the ocean, saw its waves, and a bitter hatred rose up in him.

He was about to turn away and go on back home.

Away from all this.

But then he said to himself, Why hate the sea?

Why, Paul?

It was you who killed her.

You.

She loved the sea. Loved it with her very soul.

You know that, Paul. How well you know that.

Why, she came out of the sea as if she were born in it. Like a goddess. A Greek goddess.

He began to walk slowly along the edge of the beach and to listen to the gentle sound of the waves as they rolled in to shore, a gentle, soothing sound.

"Jody," he whispered.

And suddenly she was back with him again, in the days before it all happened, the days of brightness and joy.

And he knew then that she had never left him, never disappeared from his fevered consciousness, even for the slightest instant.

Even during the bleak stretches of time when he didn't even remember her existence, when he thought he had blotted her out of his life.

You never left me, Jody. Never.

And for the first time since it happened, he felt the tears come to his eyes and streak down his cheeks.

He wept.

And a curious thing happened to him as he was weeping. He imagined for a few brief instants that she was far out in the water, in the water, her golden hair gleaming and her arms flashing in the sun.

He knew full well that it was an illusion, and yet he sat down on the hot, dry sand and watched her swim, with a glowing smile on his face and warmth and joy flooding his entire being.

Then, after those few flashing moments, moments of blazing eternity to him, she was gone from his sight and only the gleaming, undulating water remained.

Yet he sat there, in that same spot, for hours.

Still as a stone.

Just gazing out to the shimmering horizon.

And he said to himself, I know full well that it was an illusion, and so I am not mad.

Oh, Jody, I find such joy thinking of you.

Jody, Jody.

For the first time in all these agonizing and dead weeks, I feel alive once again. Alive with your love.

I know now that you did love me.

And you know how very much I loved you. With all my being.

You did know that.

You do, Jody, you do.

So you must surely forgive me.

I am certain of that now.

He watched a black freighter making its slow way south to distant waters, its entire hull wrapped gently with sun and a thin wisp of smoke curling up from its black stack and losing itself in the blue sky above, and he thought of the soft times he had spent with Jody.

He relived again all the moments, the hours.

Her sitting across the table from him, sipping coffee and smiling gently at him, the light deep in her green eyes.

Then he saw the two of them high on the stand with the night sea all about them and the dawn soon, soon to break over them, ruddy and joyous.

Her sitting high on the Ferris wheel, alone and stranded against a hostile dark sky.

Her eyes staring with poignant yearning out to where the sea began.

"Jody," he whispered. "Jody, you came out of the shining

sun and the water. The glistening green water."

His voice was lost in the vast silence.

He sat listening to the mellow thunder of the sea.

It was late afternoon when he left the beach reluctantly and turned again toward his home.

Chapter
15

He walked with a gentle smile on his lips and a glow in his eyes.

The sun shining on his tall, bronzed body.

The face clear featured, with hazel eyes.

Large, oval, hazel eyes set deep above high cheekbones.

"Paul, you are a Greek god," Jody whispered to him.

He still heard the sound of the ocean, soft in his ears.

"A Greek god," she murmured, her lips close to his.

He walked on, seeing nobody around him.

The sun was high and solid against a vast blue sky.

Chapter
16

When his feet touched the wooden steps of his house, the smile left his lips and the glow died in his eyes.

He went in and was about to go upstairs to his room when his mother came out of the kitchen.

"Paul?"

"Yes?"

"Did you eat already?" she asked.

He stood looking at her and couldn't remember.

"Did you?"

"I guess not," he said.

And then he remembered that he hadn't eaten for hours. Yet he didn't feel hungry at all.

"Shall I make you something?"

"Okay."

"Anything special you want?"

"No, Mom. Just what's easiest for you."

He started up the stairs when she called up to him.

"Paul."

He turned on the landing.

"Yes?"

"I almost forgot. There was a call for you."

"Who?"

"A girl."

"What's her name?"

"Jody."

He put his hand on the banister and held it tight.

"What?"

"That's what she said."

"You mean Joan," he said.

His mother shook her head. "I know Joan's voice by this time."

He slowly came down the stairs again.

"What did you say her name was?" he asked.

"Jody."

He breathed in and then spoke quietly. "Mother, stop playing around with me. I'm not in the mood."

"I don't know what you mean by that," she said.

"That was not her name."

"I tell you it was," she insisted.

"No," he said.

"Paul, she called three times."

"Three?"

"Yes. And each time she said to make sure you knew it was Jody calling."

He slowly sat down on the stairs and didn't speak.

"I asked if you could call her back," she continued.

He looked questioningly up at her.

"And?"

"She said you knew her number. That she was staying at the same motel."

His face had become white and tense.

"Paul, what is it?" she asked.

He shook his head and didn't answer her.

"Please tell me."

"It's nothing," he muttered.

"You don't look well."

"I'm all right," he said grimly. "This is somebody's idea of a joke."

"A joke?"

62

"I don't know who it can be. But it's sick."

He sat there silently.

"Paul," she said, as she came closer to him, her face tight with anxiety.

"Paul, who is Jody?"

At the sound of the name, he suddenly looked coldly up at his mother. But he didn't speak.

"You never spoke of her before," she said.

"I didn't."

"She evidently means a lot to you."

"She does."

"Paul, who is she?"

"Jody belongs to me," he said harshly.

She drew back. "What?"

"To me and to no one else," he said.

"What are you saying?"

But he wasn't listening to her anymore.

"Don't ever ask me about her again. Do you hear?" he said, almost angrily.

"Paul."

His hands clenched and unclenched.

"Don't ever do it, Mother."

"I don't understand," she said.

"You don't have to. Just don't ever ask me about her again. You or Dad or anybody else in this God's world."

"Paul!"

His voice rose. "Never!"

He got up and went out of the house.

Chapter
17

He went into the phone booth and called the motel.

"Have you a Jody Miller registered there?"

There was a pause and then he heard, "Yes."

"Are you sure?" said Paul.

"Jody Miller. Is that the name?" asked the clerk.

"Not a Joan, maybe? Or something close to it?"

"No. Jody," the clerk answered.

"That's it," Paul said.

"She's registered here."

"What room is she in?"

"107."

Paul gasped.

It was the same room she had the last time, he thought.

Nobody in this town knew that but he and Jody.

He had told no one.

"Do you want to talk to her?" asked the clerk.

Paul stood there and didn't speak.

"Well?"

"Yes," he whispered.

"I can't hear you."

"Yes," Paul said and his voice sounded loud and strange to him.

He heard the ringing and felt himself grow cold all over as he heard the receiver being picked up and then a voice.

"Hello?"

It was not Jody's voice.

He breathed out in relief.

"Yes? What do you want?" The voice was cold and brassy.

"Is Jody Miller there?" he said.

"Who?"

"Jody Mill—"

"You have the wrong room," the woman cut in.

"I'm sorry," he said.

"You should be."

There was a sharp click.

He stood there a while in the booth, and then he closed the doors and called the motel again.

"Jody Miller, please."

"Okay."

He heard the ringing, but this time nobody picked up the receiver.

"She doesn't answer."

"Are you sure it's the right room? You gave me the wrong one the last time."

"Oh, did I? I'm sorry. I'm ringing one-oh-seven," said the clerk.

"You sure this time?"

"Yes."

Paul listened to the persistent ringing.

"I'm afraid she's not in her room," the man said.

"Looks like it."

"Do you want to leave a message?"

"No," Paul said and hung up.

He felt himself stifling in the closed booth, yet he didn't open the doors but just stood there.

Finally he stepped out into the warm evening air.

His forehead was wet with perspiration, wet and cold.

Chapter

18

He felt that he had to see someone, to talk, just to say words to another human being. Just that and nothing more. Something to quiet the turmoil that was now inside him.

So he walked over to Ralph's house, then went up the driveway to the back, and found him sitting on a chair, under a tree, smoking a cigarette and listening to some music.

He motioned Paul to a chair and smiled at him.

Paul sat down and looked over at his friend, and a yearning came over him. A yearning to be like Ralph, who took life so easily, without breaking stride no matter what happened to him.

Long, lean, and red haired with gray, smiling eyes.

Always had it smooth.

Ralph's father was a successful corporation lawyer who went into New York every day to his big office and came home at the same time in the early evening.

His mother always busy with social and charitable affairs.

His two sisters, just as smooth and pleasant, settled in two top colleges, now away visiting relatives in Newport.

Ralph took summer jobs just to keep up the pretense of

doing something useful. Even selling ice cream was useful to him.

"I feel that I'm part of the social and economic system, if you know what I mean, Paul."

And Paul looked hard to see the sardonic gleam in Ralph's gray eyes, but he couldn't find it.

All he did know was that Ralph would always be a winner, no matter what he did.

"What's doing, Paul?"

Paul shook his head. "Nothing much."

"Status quo?"

"Yes."

"Up periscope and all that jazz?" said Ralph.

"All that jazz."

"Then you're ahead of the game," Ralph smiled.

"I guess I am."

He had known Ralph since childhood, and he suddenly became aware that he really knew nothing about him. Nothing that really counted.

And it was the same with Ralph toward him.

There was his friend smiling warmly at him, jesting with him, and not being able to see the torture and the fear that were inside him.

Can't you see it, Ralph?

Isn't it clear to you?

Doesn't it even show in my eyes?

In my voice?

Don't you feel it?

And then he heard Ralph's easy voice. "Want to go anywhere? I'm free."

Paul shrugged and murmured, "I'm not in the mood."

"Let's call up Jane."

"Jane?"

"I'll call up Jane and you call Joan. How about it?" said Ralph.

"No," Paul said.

"Jane and Joan. The two Js. I like them both."

"You like the world," Paul said.

Ralph laughed. "Do I?"

"Yes."

"I like it because the world likes me," Ralph said.

"That makes sense."

And Paul laughed, too.

But he wanted to cry, Ralph, I need you. I need you badly. I want to open up to you and talk. Help me, Ralph.

"You know, Joan always asks me about you," Ralph said.

"Does she?"

Ralph nodded. "She likes you an awful lot. Even dreams about you."

"Does she?"

"Uh-huh. Wants to see you more often."

And Paul suddenly leaned over to his friend, his face tense. "Ralph, listen to me."

"Sure."

"Turn off the music, will you?" Paul said sharply.

Ralph looked quietly at him and shut off the music. "Go on," he said.

"Is it possible for someone dead to . . . to. . . ."

And he stopped and didn't go on.

"To do what?" asked Ralph.

Paul suddenly waved his hand despondently.

"Oh, it's a crock. Forget it."

"You want to say something. Say it, Paul."

Paul shook his head. "No."

"You sure you don't want to talk about it?"

"I'm sure."

Ralph turned away from him and looked out onto the slow-coming night. Paul sat back in his chair silently.

And he wanted to say to Ralph, I need you. Yet he found that he couldn't do it.

He wondered why.

And then he said to himself, We sit in our private cells our whole life long. Isn't that how it is when it comes down to the bone, to the essential nature of things? Isn't it?

68

Look at my mother. What do I know about her? The real person? What?

My quiet, withdrawn father?

I mean the things that really count in their lives. Don't they shut themselves away from us as I do from them?

Isn't the whole world that way?

Take my sister Jean, who is so close to me, closer than anybody else. Do I know why she doesn't marry the fellow she lives with on and off? Did she ever come to me and. . . . ?

Cells.

Our little private cells.

Which become at times our private hells.

As mine is now.

He rose to his feet.

"I think I'll move on," he said.

"You don't want to go out?"

"Not tonight."

"Not tonight, Josephine," Ralph said.

"That's about it," Paul smiled.

"Take care."

"I will."

And then Ralph said it again. "Take care, Paul."

Paul looked at him and their eyes met, and then he turned and left his friend.

Chapter
19

He wandered about aimlessly and now the night had come on, a still, windless night. A slim crescent of moon was high in the sky.

He turned down a dark, tree-lined block near his home, and he stopped stock-still. A figure was standing near the trunk of an old tree, a slight sheen of moonlight on her golden hair.

She stood there, waiting for him.

"Jody," he whispered.

And then he started to walk rapidly toward her, but when he got closer hea saw it was not Jody at all.

He walked past the girl, his heart still beating rapidly.

I've got to watch myself, he said.

I've got to.

Chapter

20

Someone's playing a trick on me, a cruel trick.

Mean and cruel.

Sick.

But who would do such a thing to me?

And why?

Why?

It's such a vicious trick, so heartless.

But then the phone rang. It was eleven o'clock that night, and he was alone in the house. His parents had gone to a movie.

He was sitting in the living room, sitting alone in the darkness. Brooding.

Paul let the phone ring, hoping that it would stop, but it didn't and finally he went over to it and picked up the receiver.

And at that instant a strange image came stealthily into his mind. An image of the gulls sitting on the beach, sitting in a cluster in the hot, shining sun, their dark eyes glittering.

Sitting motionlessly and waiting endlessly. Like a dark, inevitable fate.

Then the image silently and swiftly sped away.

His hand held the receiver, loosely.

"Hello?" he said.

And then he heard his name.

"Paul?"

He trembled all over.

"Jody?"

It was her voice, her voice.

"Oh, it's so good to hear you, Paul. So wonderfully good."

He stood there silent, completely silent.

It was her voice.

No one in the world could fool him on that.

It was Jody.

"Paul, speak to me. Please."

Now he felt a chill racing through him, an icy, piercing chill.

He shivered, his hands trembled, and he dropped the phone onto the wooden part of the floor, the part not covered by the rug. It made a deep and hollow sound that seemed to echo throughout the empty, dark house. He listened to it. A hollow, silvery sound.

Then he slowly stooped and picked up the receiver again.

He put it to his ear. It felt cold, icy cold.

"Paul. Paul, are you there?"

Her voice was so desperate and so eager.

"Yes," he whispered.

"Don't go away," she said.

"I won't."

"Please."

"I won't," he said again.

He looked through the open window and saw the plane tree that stood on the front of the lawn. Old and lean and shadowy in the darkness. Saw its leaves shake and quiver in a soft breeze. His senses were so sharpened that he felt he could hear the sound they made in the still night.

He kept looking through the window at the tinkling leaves.

Then he heard her voice again. "Please speak to me. I've

72

been away and it's been so bleak without you."

So bleak.

So desolate.

"Speak to me," she said.

Suddenly he found that he couldn't talk.

"Say my name. Please say my name."

"I . . . can't," he said.

"You must."

"I . . . I. . . ."

"For my sake. Say it."

"Jo. . . ."

"You don't know how important it is to me. Say the name."

He made a great effort.

"Jody," he said.

He heard her sigh and it almost brought tears to his eyes.

"Oh, Paul. Paul."

He felt his knees begin to shake violently. He sat down heavily on a chair.

"Paul."

It was Jody's voice, he said over and over to himself. There is no other voice in the world like hers.

"Paul, listen to me."

"Yes?"

"Say 'Yes, Jody,' " she said. He heard her sigh again. "Oh, Paul. I must see you again. I must or I shall die."

And then her voice went on.

"I love you, Paul. More than I ever did. If that is possible."

If that is possible, he thought desperately.

"But everything is possible in this world. Isn't it, Paul? Isn't it?"

He didn't speak.

"Talk to me. I hunger so for your voice. To see you again. To look into your hazel eyes. Oh, I have so much to tell you. I've been so far, far away but now I'm back. I'm back, Paul."

You are back, he thought.

And he kept looking at the tree and hearing the shaking leaves. Like soft, silvery bells.

The night had become so dark. The slip of moon had disappeared into the clouds.

I'm being haunted, he said to himself.

It must be that. It can't be anything else.

Haunted.

These things do happen.

I know that now.

I do.

He heard Jody speak to him again.

"I shall never leave you. Never."

"Jody."

"Paul, I must see you."

"See me?" he said, as the chill began to spread over him again.

"Tonight."

"What?"

"I can't wait. I must see your face again."

"Jody."

"I want to be in your arms again."

And suddenly he cried out.

"Please, Jody. Leave me in peace."

He heard her gasp and it cut through him.

"You must," he said.

"Peace? Why do you say that to me? Why?"

He didn't answer.

"Why do you tear my heart this way?" she cried.

"Jody, I. . . ."

And he couldn't go on.

"This is so cruel and unfair to me."

He looked out at the still and lone tree, standing so forlornly in the darkness, and then he heard her speak to him again.

This time her voice was low and sad, and it seemed to him to come from a chill distance.

"You do me great harm this way, Paul."

"Harm? No. No."

"You do."

"Jody, I wouldn't hurt you for anything in this world. You know that."

She was silent.

"You always knew that," he said.

"Then see me tonight."

"But—"

"Tonight, Paul." Her voice became soft and insistent.

He thrilled just to hear its subtle melody.

"Come to me. Meet me at the Ferris wheel."

"The wheel?"

"Yes, Paul. Yes."

"It's closed at this hour. Past the season. Closes early."

"I know. I know. But I spoke to the man and he says he'll keep it open just for me. For me."

"You spoke to him?"

"Yes. It'll be just like the first time, Paul."

"Just like the first time," he said mechanically.

"Do you remember?"

And he saw her sitting against the night sky, her hair glowing.

"Yes, Jody," he murmured.

"I'll wait there for you."

"When?"

"In a half hour."

"Jody, I. . . ."

His voice died out and he stood there in a bewildered silence. Then he heard her speak to him again.

"Paul."

"Yes?"

"Will you be there?"

He didn't answer.

"I will," she said.

He heard her put down the phone.

A chill breeze came up and shook the leaves of the tree,

again and again. He heard once more the sound of soft silver bells.

The slim crescent of moon showed itself from behind the slow, scudding clouds. A thin, cold gleam.

He sat there looking at it and listening to the silvery leaves.

Listening.

I'm haunted, he said to himself.

Haunted.

Chapter

21

He remembered reading in *Hamlet* the line, "For this way lies madness."

This way.

Paul sat there in the silent house, not moving.

I should not go to see her.

She won't be there anyway.

And if she is?

For this way lies madness.

This way.

Then he slowly got up and sighed and opened the door and walked out into the night.

The leaves of the tree were still.

Deathly still.

Chapter

22

He walked along the deserted and darkened amusement area, the night quiet around him. From the distance he could hear the murmur of the sea, low and enchanting, weaving gently through his being, like a melody.

He walked.

Past the gaunt steel skeleton of the parachute jump, past the silent and dead Cyclone, and then he came to the Ferris wheel.

He saw its lightless form, the gleam of moonlight falling upon its arc, and then he stopped.

His lips dropped open.

He felt his heart race.

For there, sitting as he had first seen her, on a swinging seat, stranded against the dark sky, was Jody.

She wore the very same clothes. A light silk blouse, gray summer slacks. Her golden hair was drawn back into a bun.

She had not seen him yet.

She sat there, staring out to where the sea began, a poignant, searching look in her eyes.

A great warmth spread through him as he stood there looking up at her. And it seemed to him that the darkness of the night had lifted just a bit.

Just enough for him to see the sheen of her hair.

"Jody," he whispered.

Then he drew a step closer to the wheel and she saw him.

"Paul." Her voice floated down to him.

She said his name again.

He could now see her face, her eyes, her lips.

"It is you, Jody," he said.

Her sea green eyes.

"It is."

She smiled down at him.

"Yes," he said. "Yes."

"You came. I knew you would come."

"I had to," he said.

"I'm back, Paul. You can see that now, can't you?"

"Yes. And you won't leave me again."

"Never."

He stood looking up at her, his eyes bright and shining, a glow within him.

"I have my Greek god again," she said.

Then for a brief, vibrant instant they were silent, as if poised in time and space. As if everything had stopped.

Then he stirred himself.

"Jody, come down to me," he said.

"Shall I?"

And there was a gentle and mischievous look in the green eyes.

"Stop playing with me."

"All right, Paul," she smiled.

"Tell me what to do."

"The lever, Paul. As simple as that."

"What?"

"That's all there is to it. The man said just pull the lever and I will come down to you."

"Are you sure?"

"Of course."

He turned to where she was pointing and he saw a series of levers. He turned back to her.

"Did he say which one?"

"The first, Paul. The first one on your right. It's so simple. I saw him do it. Simple, Paul."

Paul put his hand to the lever but it would not move.

"What's wrong, Paul?"

He used all his strength but it would not budge an inch.

He looked up desperately at her.

"It's locked."

"But it can't be."

"I tell you it is."

"Are you sure? Try again," she said.

He shook his head.

"No use, Jody."

She put her hand out, and he could see it flash an instant and then lose itself in the upper darkness.

"Then you'll have to get him."

"Where? Where is he?" he asked.

"At the coffee shop on West Street. He said he'd be there."

Paul stood there and didn't move.

He heard her speak to him again.

"His name is Morgan. A short, gray-haired man. Said he knew you, Paul."

"I don't know him," Paul said coldly.

"Go anyway. Please."

He stood there looking up at her, and the glow was dying within him. And only black despair was coming in after it. Black, hopeless despair.

"What is it, Paul?"

There was fear in her face now.

"I don't want to leave you here," he said.

"Why?"

"I'll lose you again."

She shook her head. "You'll never lose me again."

He didn't speak.

"Please go and get him. Please, Paul."

He looked despairingly up at her, and he saw the tears start in her eyes and it cut him to the heart.

"Jody."

"You know I love you."

"Yes."

"I will never leave you again. Believe me."

"I do believe you," he said.

"Then go."

He still stood there.

"What is it now?"

"You said West Street?"

"Yes."

"You're sure?"

"The coffee shop."

"I know it," he said.

"Hurry, Paul. It's getting so cold up here."

But the night was hot and still.

"Yes, Jody," he said.

He turned abruptly and hurried down the long and dark alley. He paused an instant and turned back and he saw her sitting there, her eyes staring out to where the sea began.

Chapter
23

When he came to the coffee shop it was closed.

Dark and closed.

Paul stood there bewildered and lost.

He swung around suddenly and raced down the echoing alleys, his feet thudding against the silence.

He came in sight of the Ferris wheel again.

He stopped and a low cry burst from him.

"Jody!"

There was no one sitting on the wheel.

She was gone.

Gone.

And only the dark night remained.

Chapter

24

He heard a voice from behind him.

"Are you Paul?"

He turned and saw the figure come out from the shadows and approach him.

"Yes?"

It was a man, short and gray haired.

"I have a message for you," the man said.

"What is it?"

The man's voice was quiet and low against the night when he spoke again.

"Jody said she had to go away."

"Where?"

"She didn't tell me."

Paul stared at the man.

"She said she couldn't help it. She had to go."

Paul didn't speak.

"I'm Morgan," the man said.

"You saw her?"

"Yes."

"You spoke to her?"

"Yes."

The man's eyes were quietly studying Paul.

"You let her go up on the wheel?"

"Yes."

"You brought her down?"

The man nodded silently.

"Why?"

"It was to please you. She gave me thirty dollars."

"To please me?"

"Just seeing her up there again. Against the night sky."

"She said that?"

"She said that," the man echoed.

From the distance Paul could hear the murmur of the sea, the low, enchanting murmur. He listened to it with his whole being.

"She's a very beautiful girl. Out of this world," the man said.

"Yes."

Paul glanced away from the man and looked up at the lightless wheel.

A gentle, thin gleam lay upon its silent arc, then slowly filtered down onto the empty seat where Jody once sat.

The seat still seemed to be swinging.

Softly swinging.

And for a fervent instant he could have sworn that he could see her still sitting there and gazing out to where the sea began.

Jody, he whispered within.

The warmth spread through him again and he smiled.

But then he looked away from the dark wheel and down at the man and saw the cold glint of light that was on his narrow face and gray hair.

It didn't happen, he said to himself. It couldn't have.

This way lies madness.

"Where did she go?" he said.

The man shook his head.

"She didn't tell me."

"Which way did she walk?"

"Toward the beach."

"Are you sure?"

"Yes."

Paul stood there silently, listening to the murmur of the distant sea.

The man turned and began to walk back into the darkness from which he had come.

"Wait," Paul said.

The man stopped and turned.

Paul went over to him, and his steps on the pavement sounded loud and hollow to his ears.

"You say you spoke to her?"

The man didn't seem surprised that Paul asked that question.

"Yes," he said quietly.

"You heard her speak to you?"

"Yes?"

"Did you touch her?"

"Touch her?" the man asked.

"Please tell me."

"When she gave me the money."

"You touched her hand?" Paul said.

"Yes."

Paul hesitated and then he spoke again.

"Was it cold?"

"Cold?" the man said.

"Or warm?"

"Warm?" he echoed.

"You're laughing at me, aren't you?" said Paul.

"No."

"You think I'm mad."

The man shook his head.

"You do," Paul said. "Because I do, too."

The man looked long and silently at Paul.

"I'm not laughing at you," he said. "Not laughing at all. I'm sorry for you, son."

Paul drew back.

"What?"

"Yes. Sorry."

And then he walked away from Paul and disappeared down one of the dark and empty alleys.

Chapter

25

He walked the beach and listened to the pulsing sound of the ocean. And as he walked, he knew that deep within him, he still desperately hoped he would find her again. That his eyes would see her once more that night.

That enchanted, haunted night.

Just once more.

To talk to her again.

To hear her soft, melodious voice.

To put his arms around her and whisper to her.

Just that.

And no more.

But then he said to himself wearily, It's hopeless. .

And mad.

He clenched his hands and stood still under the dark, starless sky.

He decided to turn away from the beach and go back to his home when suddenly a restless urge came over him, an urge to get into the water and swim far out. Restless and overpowering.

He could not fight it down.

Paul stripped on the deserted beach and then strode into

the soon-enveloping water, feeling it instantly soothe him and quiet his whole being.

He swam with strong, smooth strokes. Swam far, far out until he could no longer see the sparse lights on the shore. And the farther he swam, the more free he became.

Free from the haunting thoughts of her.

Until he became alone with the vast night and the vast, undulating sea that he loved so dearly.

Loved all his young life.

And then strange and fanciful imaginings came to him as he swam farther and farther out to the night horizon of the ocean.

A Greek god. Maybe I am a Greek god come out of the sea. Maybe centuries ago, in another existence, I was a Greek god who remained all his life in the sea.

And knew only Greek goddesses.

Knew only one.

And she. . . .

It was then that the thought of her came back into his soul.

"Jody," he whispered.

And he soon felt that she was swimming beside him.

Silently.

And with such quiet love.

Chapter
26

But when he stepped out of the water and onto the beach again, his body white and dripping in the warm darkness, he knew it was all an illusion. A desperate and mad illusion.

Jody is dead, the harsh waves told him over and over.

Dead.

Dead.

You did not see her or meet her tonight.

You did not talk to her.

You did not swim with her.

It was not Jody.

It couldn't be.

Someone is creating a cruel illusion for you. And you with your fevered and sick imagination are helping it all along.

Somehow, someone is tricking you.

Face it, you poor fool.

Jody is dead.

Dead.

The dead do not come back.

Never.

Never.

Never.

Paul put his hands to his ears to drown out the sound of the brutal, crashing waves.

Finally, he let his hands fall to his sides.

He dressed and went through the night to his home. And as he walked down the final tree-lined street he felt that someone had begun to follow him.

With soft, smooth steps.

He stopped and the sound of the footsteps faded away.

Paul turned sharply and peered down the long, silent block but he saw no one.

Only a faint shadow of a form standing by a huge elm tree.

He stood looking at it for a long moment.

The shadow did not move.

He turned and began to walk on again, and he heard once more the footsteps on the dark pavement.

Soft, ever so soft.

As if the walker wore ballet shoes.

Paul stopped and whirled around.

"Jody," he called out, his voice ringing through the night.

But no one answered.

Chapter
27

He slept badly the few remaining hours of that night.

And he dreamed.

He watched Joe Carson come slowly into his room, and then take a chair and move it close to the bed and sit down on it and just gaze mournfully into his face.

"What is it, Joe?" Paul asked.

"I'm worried about you."

"Why?"

"Because you committed a crime."

"I know."

"You could have saved her. It was easy. And you lost her," Joe said.

Paul didn't speak.

"You should have been in the water much sooner."

"I know."

Joe Carson looked long at Paul.

"Crimes must be punished," he finally said.

"Must they?"

"I'm afraid so, son."

"Joe."

"Yes?"

"Why do you call me son?"

"Because I never had one."

"And I . . . ?"

"You are the son I never had."

"I disappointed you," Paul said in a low voice.

"You did."

"I'm terribly sorry, Joe."

He saw Joe shake his head sadly.

"It's no use, Paul. You'll have to pay for your crime."

"But I didn't mean it."

Carson shook his head. "No defense."

"You know I didn't mean it. You do, Joe."

"I know nothing."

"In your heart, you do. You know me so well," Paul said.

"What's in your heart or mine doesn't count. You committed a crime."

"Please, Joe."

Carson shook his close-cropped head. His voice became hard when he spoke again.

"There's nothing I can do about it. It's out of my hands."

Paul leaned forward to the man, a great plea in his eyes.

"I loved her. Still love her."

"And?"

"Loved her," Paul said again.

"We kill the things we love," Joe said.

Paul drew back and lowered his head. He could no longer look at the man.

"We do," he murmured. "We do."

There was a long silence.

It was Paul who spoke first. "Joe."

"Well?"

"Joe, tell me."

And he couldn't go on.

"Speak."

Paul tried again. "Joe, tell me. Do the dead ever come back?"

"The dead?"

Paul silently nodded and inside him was a great fear, a dread.

"You mean do they come back to this world of ours?"

Paul nodded again.

There was a silence.

Paul looked away from the man to the night that was beyond them. The darkness seemed to be pressing hard against the closed window, trying desperately to force its way into the room and envelop the two of them.

He turned back to the man.

He heard his voice, drifting in to him, as from a great distance.

"No, Paul. The dead do not come back to this world."

"Are you sure?"

"I am sure."

Paul felt a heavy weight fall away from him, and a soothing sense of relief began to spread through his being. Soothing and liberating.

But then Joe Carson looked steadily at him, his lips grim, his eyes like little bits of cold steel.

"Does it make you feel any better, Paul?"

Paul didn't answer.

"It does. I can see that it does."

"Yes," Paul whispered.

And then Carson spoke in a flat, harsh voice.

"But the murdered dead do come back. They alone do."

Paul drew away from him.

"It's not so."

A cold gleam came into the man's eyes.

"They do, Paul. Especially when their killer walks free. Then they come back. With a vengeance."

"No," Paul moaned. "No."

"Yes, my son. Yes."

And then Paul woke up, and the sun was streaming into the room.

Chapter
28

When he called the motel in the morning, he was told she had checked out.

"Jody Miller? Room 107?"

"Yes."

"When was that?"

"Late last night," said the clerk.

"Did she leave any forwarding address?"

"No."

"And were there any messages?"

"Only one. For a Paul Barrett."

"I'm Paul Barrett."

"It's in a sealed envelope," the man said.

"Could you open it and read it to me?"

"Okay."

There was a pause and then he heard the man's voice again.

"I just glanced at it. It's very personal. Are you sure you want me to read it?"

"Please," Paul said.

"All right."

The man paused again and then Paul heard him read the message aloud.

"Paul, how could you be so cruel? How? Why didn't you come back? I waited and waited. How could you do this to me? Now I know that you don't care anymore. That's why you let me die."

The man paused and then went on.

"I'm going away. Forever. Jody."

Paul stood there and didn't move.

Then he heard the man's voice.

"Well?"

"Are you sure that's the message? There's no mistake?"

"I just read it to you, young man."

"Yes. I'm sorry."

"That's all right. I understand."

The voice was elderly and tolerant.

"Could I hold you just a minute longer? Please. It's very important to me."

"Go ahead."

"Did you ever see Jody Miller?"

"See her? Yes. When she checked in and a few times after that."

"Are you sure it was Jody Miller?"

"Of course I am. I remember her from her last stay. She's not very easy to forget. Not at all, young man."

"Is she very beautiful and wears her hair in a bun? Golden hair?"

"That's Miss Miller."

"And she has that walk that ballet dancers have?"

He heard a low, amused laugh. "Yes, if that's how you put it."

"The last question. Please."

"What is it?"

"Did you see her last night?"

"Yes."

"What time?"

"About ten or a little later."

"She was leaving the motel?"

"Yes."

95

"Please. Was she wearing a light silk blouse and gray slacks?"

"Yes. She was. Very attractive in it, too."

Paul stood there silently.

"Any more questions?"

Paul didn't answer.

"Well?"

Paul was now able to speak.

"No. Thanks very much."

And then he hung up and walked out of the phone booth, his face pale and ashen.

Chapter
29

He was walking along one of the neat and quiet streets of his town in the early afternoon, when a car pulled up to the curb near him and he heard his name called.

He turned and walked slowly over to the car.

"Hello, Joan," he said.

In a way he was glad to see her.

"What are you doing, Paul?"

He shrugged his broad shoulders.

"Nothing. Nothing much."

"How about taking a ride?" she asked.

He hesitated.

"I don't know."

"We're both doing nothing. Let's make something."

"I don't know," he said again.

"Why not?"

"Okay, Joan."

He got into the car beside her and she drove off, out of the town and onto the highway.

The sun was high above them.

"Anyplace you want to go?"

The top of the car was down and the cooling air swept over him.

"You pick it," he said.

"How about Cranford Mall?"

"The mall?"

"We'll walk around and then have something to eat," she said.

"Sure."

"Doesn't matter, does it?"

She smiled, but her eyes were studying him.

"It doesn't," he said.

"You haven't much to say these days, Paul."

"I guess I haven't."

"You never did say much."

"I didn't."

"But now you practically say nothing at all."

"Do I?"

She nodded. "You seem to be in another world."

He didn't speak for a while, and then he said in a low, brooding voice, "Maybe I am."

And then he said it again.

She looked sharply at him.

"What do you mean by that, Paul?"

He sighed low and shrugged. "Who knows?"

"Paul."

"Yes?"

"Do you want to talk about it?"

He shook his head. "No."

"You sure?"

"Yes."

"But I would like to—"

He softly cut in.

"Let it alone, Joan."

"Okay."

He reached over and touched her hand gently.

"Thanks, anyway."

"Right, Paul," she smiled.

Then she was quiet for a while, concentrating on the heavy traffic that was now ahead of her.

He sat there studying her profile and he thought to himself, She is a very good-looking girl. Auburn hair, fair skin, blue eyes, and a warm smile.

A smile that is always there, mostly in the eyes.

She likes life.

A good person.

It's always very pleasant being with her.

Always was.

And then he thought to himself, If Jody hadn't come along maybe something would've developed between Joan and me.

Who knows?

But Jody did come along.

He put his head back against the seat rest and closed his eyes. He felt the cooling breeze upon him.

The rays of the hot sun falling softly onto his hair and face.

The day still and silent around him.

Suddenly the image of the gulls slid into his consciousness and he saw them again.

He, sitting high on the lifeguard stand, and they below him, clustered and still.

Their black eyes staring up at him.

Like grim fate, he thought.

I shall never escape my fate.

Never.

"Paul."

He slowly opened his eyes.

"We're there," Joan said.

And my fate is to go mad, he thought.

Chapter

30

She walked along the mall with him and she got him smiling again.

"Getting hungry?"

"A little, Joan."

"So am I. What do you feel like having?"

They had come to the food rotunda of the mall and stood at its center, under the high glass cupola, looking around them at the different stalls, bright and varicolored, that offered many varieties of fast food.

"You choose, Joan."

She smiled.

"No, you."

"You."

They both laughed together.

"Chinese," she said.

"Good enough."

She shook her head.

"That was too quick a choice. You have to think it out. How about Tex-Mex?"

"Okay."

"Still too quick," she said.

"Whatever you want."

"We're back to where we started. Pizza."

"Sure."

"You're too easy to please," she laughed.

"Always was," he chuckled.

He was feeling light headed, as if he had drunk some wine.

"We'll toss a coin," he said.

"For what?"

"Tex-Mex or pizza."

He took out a quarter and tossed it into the air and then deftly caught it in his big palm.

He closed his fist over the coin.

"Call," he said to her.

"Heads."

"Okay."

"And what happens if it is heads?" she asked.

"I don't know."

They both laughed.

And again he felt as if he had drunk wine.

He opened his hand and it was heads.

"Well?" he said to her.

"Tex-Mex."

They went over to the counter, and as they stood waiting for their order to be filled, he put his arm around her shoulder.

She flushed and looked up at him.

"It's good to be with you, Paul," she said in a low and tremulous voice.

And he realized how much and how desperately she cared for him.

"Good to be with you, Joan," he murmured.

He wanted to take his arm away, but he did not want to hurt her.

He let it stay there.

Joan, he said to himself, it's too late for us. Can't you see that? Jody has come in and taken my life away with her.

There's nothing I can do about that.

Nothing.

You must understand, you must.

And try to forget me.

"Paul?"

"Yes?"

"Let's sit close to the music. Okay?"

"Sure, Joan. Whatever you want."

She paused and looked up at him.

"You don't mind, do you?"

"Why should I mind?"

She didn't answer him.

They made their way to the center of the area, where a slender woman with a fixed smile sat at a dark, gleaming piano playing requests from the people sitting around her.

He let Joan choose one of the inner tables, and they sat down with their trays and began to eat.

He watched her as she paused every now and then to listen to the music.

He kept looking at her softly defined profile, the glowing eyes and the partly opened lips.

She glanced over at him.

"Romantic music gets to me," she said almost defensively.

"The standards?"

"Yes."

He didn't speak.

"You don't like it, Paul?"

"I didn't say anything, Joan."

She shook her head.

"You don't care for it but you do it for me. Right?"

"Maybe."

"You're a very decent person, Paul."

"Decent?"

She nodded.

"You are. And I like you because you are."

He looked away from her.

"Did I say anything out of turn?"

He shook his head, still not looking at her.

"You didn't."

She leaned forward to him.

"Paul?"

He turned back to her.

"Yes?"

"You've stopped smiling," she said.

"Have I? I didn't realize."

She was silent for a while.

Then she spoke again.

"There's such a brooding look in your eyes now."

"Is there?"

She nodded slowly.

"Yes. Brooding and sad."

"Oh."

"What is it?"

He shook his head.

"Listen to the music and forget it," he said.

"Please, Paul."

He reached over and patted her hand.

"It's nothing, Joan. Nothing."

"But I wish you would let me—"

He cut in softly.

"Eat your taco. It's getting cold."

"What?"

Suddenly she began to laugh.

He looked at her, the gay laughter bringing a tentative smile to his face.

"What's so funny?"

"The—the way you said it. As if I were a little child. A baby."

"Oh."

"You patted my hand and said, 'Eat your taco.'"

She mimicked him.

"It was that funny?"

"Yes."

She was still laughing.

"Eat your taco," he said, mimicking himself, as if he were another person.

He began to laugh with her.

And as he did, he forgot Jody.

Forgot that she had ever lived.

Or died.

Chapter
31

The slender woman came back to the piano and sat down again. This time there was no fixed smile on her lips. Her lean, narrow face had a sad and distant look to it.

As if she had just learned some bad news.

She paused and looked over to Paul, directly at him, and was about to speak, but then her lips tightened shut.

He wondered why she had wanted to talk to him and what she would have said. For an instant, he felt a chill race through him.

And then it was gone.

The gray light of the early evening sifted down through the high glass windows and onto the lean woman and the gleaming piano.

Long and angular shadows fell across some of the inner tables, especially those near the dark piano.

The woman began to play again, soft and low. But each note was clear and distinct.

Paul and Joan sat silently listening to the music. He found himself being strangely attracted to the melodies of the old standards.

It surprised him.

He drank his coffee and then set the cup down and looked

across the table at Joan, a gentle smile in his large, hazel eyes.

"I'm glad you stopped the car and picked me up, Joan," he said.

"Are you?"

"Uh-huh."

"You looked pretty down and sort of lost," she said.

"I guess I was."

"And you feel better now?"

"Yes."

She leaned over to him.

"Paul?"

"Yes, Joan."

Her voice became low, almost hushed. "Paul, do you really like me?"

"Sure," he said.

She shook her head. "No. You say it too easily."

"Because I mean it."

"I know. But—"

"But what?"

"Paul, you know what I mean."

And he saw the desperate yearning in her eyes and was about to speak when he heard the soft music begin. A melody that he knew.

Giselle.

One of the scenes from the first act.

He listened.

And he remembered Jody showing him how she would dance that passage. And as she danced, she sang in a haunting voice.

That melody.

That very same melody.

Now it seeped into his very being like a stream of cold fire.

He shivered violently.

"Paul."

He didn't answer Joan.

"Paul, what is it? You're so pale. You're shivering."

He rose slowly from his seat and stared ahead of him.

His lips silently formed the name.

Jody.

For there at the other end of the rotunda, sitting alone at a shadowy table, sipping coffee and listening to the music with a sad and concentrated face, was Jody. Her golden hair softly glowing.

"Jody," he murmured.

"Paul, what are you saying?"

He stood there rigidly and pointed.

"Don't you see her?"

"Who?"

"At that table. The one by the gray pillar."

"See who?"

He swung around bewilderedly to Joan.

"That girl. The one with the golden hair."

"But—"

He turned away from her and pointed again.

"That girl."

Joan was now standing with him.

"But no one is there, Paul."

He looked at her.

"No one?"

"That table is empty."

And he turned again and saw that it was.

"She was there, I tell you."

"Paul, please."

There was a glisten of tears in her eyes as she put her hand tenderly on his.

"You're lying to me," he said.

"But—"

"You saw her. Just as I did."

"No, Paul. No."

His voice rose.

"Why do you do this to me? Why?"

He flung off her hand and strode away from her.

107

"Paul!"

But he did not turn.

When he came to the shadowed table, he stood there staring down at the half-empty coffee cup that still remained there.

She was here, he said to himself.

This is where she sat.

I know she did.

I could swear my life on it.

This can't be an illusion.

It mustn't be.

Her scent is in the air.

All around me.

He moved the chair, and it was then that he saw the hint of white on the gray stone floor.

The white of a small handkerchief.

He stooped and picked it up.

His fingers traced the letters that were stitched near the edge of the handkerchief.

J—O—D—Y.

He said the name.

"Jody."

He suddenly crushed the handkerchief in his fist.

"She was here," he whispered.

"Paul."

He slowly turned and looked at Joan, his face white and tense.

"Are you all right?" she asked, her lips trembling.

He didn't answer her.

"Paul, you mustn't—"

"Let's get out of here," he cut in softly. "Please, Joan."

And then he said it again, this time like a child.

"Please, Joan."

Chapter
32

As he walked away out of the shadows, Joan at his side, the piano stopped playing. The lean woman sat rigidly and stared straight ahead of her.

Soon a girl with golden hair and the walk of a ballet dancer came out from behind one of the gray pillars and walked over to the piano.

A twenty-dollar bill was in her hand.

The End

Part Three

Chapter
33

All the way home he tried to speak to Joan, but he found that he couldn't. And she didn't question him. Just sat silently at his side, her eyes intent on the road ahead of her.

It was dark when she drove down his block and stopped the car in front of his house.

He sat there a while without speaking, and then finally he turned to her.

"Joan."

"Yes, Paul?"

He hesitated and then he went on again.

"Please listen to me. Something happened when I was a lifeguard this summer. Something terrible."

"Paul, if you don't want to talk about it, don't. Please."

He shook his head desperately.

"But I *do* want to talk. I have to. I—I can't keep it in anymore."

He paused and looked around him at the dark and silent house and the trees standing quiet and alone.

And he said to himself, I'm scared to go on alone. I can't do it alone anymore. I have to tell her.

I must.

Then he heard himself speak in a low voice.

"Someone drowned."

"What?"

"It was my fault."

He saw her eyes widen, but she said nothing.

"Yes, Joan. My fault."

"No, Paul."

"Yes. Yes. I should've been out there sooner. I—I was lying on my back smoking a joint. I just lay there while she was out in the water crying for help. I just lay there in a daze and . . . and I. . . ."

His voice trembled and he couldn't go on.

"I don't believe it, Paul. Not you. No, not you."

He shook his head.

"It's true, Joan. True," he said bleakly.

A car passed by them and then slowly moved away into the deep night. They sat listening to the vanishing, desolate sound.

Then she spoke again.

"Paul."

He had not heard her the first time.

"Yes?"

"Was it a girl?"

He nodded silently.

"And did you know her?"

"Yes."

"And did you care for her?"

He bowed his head.

"Very much, Joan."

"I understand," she said in a low voice.

"Joan, I loved her."

She looked away from him and into the night.

He saw the pain in her face, and yet he had to speak.

"It's on my conscience," he said. "All the time. Even when I feel I've forgotten or repressed the whole thing. It's there. Never leaves me."

"Her name was Jody?"

He nodded.

"And you thought you saw her this evening at the mall?"

"I didn't think it."

"Paul."

"I saw her," he said intensely. "She was there. At that table."

"But that's impossible. You know it is."

"Do I?"

"You just said she was drowned."

"So?"

Her eyes anxiously searched his white face.

"Joan," he said. "I've seen her and I've spoken to her."

She trembled. "Spoken to her?"

"And she has to me."

Joan sat there staring at him.

"Yes," he said. "I tell you, yes."

His voice had begun to rise. She suddenly reached over and took his hand and held it tight.

"Paul. Paul, what are you saying?"

"The truth, Joan. The truth."

"No. This is an illusion. Can't you see that?"

He drew away from her.

"It's not."

He put his hand into his shirt pocket and drew out the handkerchief. It flashed white.

"Then what is this?" he asked harshly.

She didn't speak.

"This handkerchief with her name on it. Her name," he said insistently.

"Where did you get it?"

"Under the table. I found it under the table. She had dropped it there."

"Dropped it?"

"Yes."

She was silent.

"Well? You don't say anything now. Do you?"

His voice was harsh and challenging.

"Paul, listen to me."

"Go on," he said curtly.

"Someone is playing a horrible trick on you."

"What?"

And within he felt a chill.

Yet he waved his hand in a gesture of denial.

"It's not so."

"I tell you, it has to be."

"No," he said.

"Paul, there is no other explanation."

"Why not?" he said.

Yet the chill was still within him.

"Because any other is that of a—"

"Of a sick mind?"

"I didn't say that."

"You didn't have to. It was there just the same."

"Paul, please!"

He turned and opened the door of the car and got out.

"Thanks for the ride," he said.

"Paul, don't go off this way."

"It was a mistake to talk to you."

"It wasn't. We can still—"

"A mistake," he said bitterly.

Then he went up the front steps and into his house.

Chapter
34

He slept fitfully, the handkerchief clutched in his fist, and he dreamed.

He dreamed that Jody came into the room and stood by his bed, just staring at him a long, long time.

Her green eyes cold.

So very cold.

The love for him gone out of them.

"I've come for the handkerchief."

"Why?"

"Because it's mine."

"I'd like to keep it."

"No."

"Just as a remembrance of you."

"Our love is over," she said.

"Why, Jody?"

"Because you are starting to forget me," she said.

"Forget? Never."

"You are and you will. The living forget the dead."

"No. That's not so."

"That's how life is. You'll find new interests. New loves."

"I'll always remember you," he said.

"You lie."

"I never lied to you."

"There's always a first time. And this is it, Paul."

She suddenly reached over and snatched the handkerchief from his grip.

"Jody!" he cried out. "Please let me keep it."

And then he heard her laugh harshly.

"But it's not yours to keep, Paul."

"Please. I'll die without it, Jody."

She laughed again.

"You're going to die anyway, Paul. With it or without it. For your sin."

"No."

"You're going to kill yourself. Can't you see that?"

"Jody, please...."

He held out his hand pleadingly to her, but she moved back and vanished into the darkness.

He awoke and saw a shadowy figure standing by his bed.

"Jody?"

"It's me, Paul."

His mother was standing near him, the handkerchief in her hand.

"You called out to me," she said.

He stared at her.

"A few times, Paul."

"I did?"

"When I came in, you said something about a handkerchief. It was on the floor."

He was silent.

"Paul, what's wrong?"

"I'm okay, Mother," he said.

"Are you?"

"Please don't crowd me. I told you I'm all right."

"But, Paul...."

He reached up and touched her hand.

"Better go back to sleep," he said, his voice gentle now. "I'm sorry I woke you up."

She stood there hesitant and vulnerable, still wanting to stay at his side.

Suddenly he felt a great compassion for her.

"Mom," he said.

"Yes?"

And he wanted to say to her, I'm sorry for some of the harsh things I've said to you, Mom. I'm not myself these days.

Forgive me. I should be more tender with you.

I should.

I know you've had your share of disappointments in this life. Dad was and is a disaster to you. And Jean drives you up the wall with her life-style.

I know it all, Mom.

He kept looking at his mother without speaking.

And he thought with a great sadness, Where did your beauty go?

Where?

I remember it so well. As a child, I was so proud of my beautiful mother.

So proud.

But he did not say the words he wanted to say to her.

"Better go back to bed, Mom."

"Would you like me to sit and talk a while?"

He shook his head.

"No, Mom."

"Are you sure?"

"Yes."

"Paul."

"Well?"

And he knew that at that instant she wanted to say things to him.

Things that were in her heart.

Years ago when he was twelve, she used to confide in him all her inner dreams and heartbreaks.

Only to him.

And then she suddenly stopped.

He never knew why.

"Try to sleep, Paul," she said.

"I will."

Then he saw her put the handkerchief on the night table and slowly go out of the room.

Chapter
35

He was sitting on the porch looking out at the sunlight filtering through the green leaves of the plane tree, the sea green leaves, when he heard the phone ring in the living room.

He got up slowly and went inside.

And the instant he put his cold hand to the receiver, he knew who the caller was.

"Jody?"

"Yes. This is Miss Miller."

The voice was low and harsh, like that of the Jody of the dream.

"Miss Miller?"

"Jody Miller."

There was a short silence.

Then he heard her voice again.

"First you kill and then you betray."

"What?"

"The girl you were with in the mall. I followed you there. I follow you all the time, Paul."

"Jody, I—"

"You love her, don't you, Hazel Eyes?"

"No."

"Liar."

"Jody, I like her a lot. That's all there is to it."

"Of course."

"I'm telling you the truth," he said.

"Are you?"

"Yes."

"I've come to hate you, Paul," she said bitterly.

"Hate me? No. Never, Jody."

"Yes, Paul. Hate. Bitter, burning hatred. I had a chance to come back and share a life with you. But now you've destroyed it."

"That's not so."

"It is."

He stood there silent. The room seemed to be closing in on him, and then he heard her voice again.

"You'll pay for your crime, Paul. Believe me, you will."

"No."

And then her voice became a hoarse whisper.

"The water covered my lips, my eyes, and then my golden hair, and I cried out to you for help. To you, my lover. But you did not come."

"I didn't hear you," he said.

"You did. In your soul you know that you did."

"Please. Please believe me."

"You let me drown. Out there in the darkening water."

As he stood there, trembling, he could almost see her shaking her wet, golden head.

Shaking it grimly, bitterly, the water dripping down her face and onto the white dry sand.

"You lie," the voice whispered hoarsely. "You didn't come and I'm dead. Forever dead."

He could see her dead eyes staring at him.

Coldly piercing into him.

"Dead. But I'm back from the darkening water. Back to torture you."

And suddenly he heard himself cry out from the depths of his being, "Who are you?"

There was a silence.

"Who?" he cried out again.

His voice echoed throughout the empty house.

Outside the air was still, deathly still.

And then he heard the chilling voice float in to him.

"Jody Miller."

"No."

"Yes, dear Paul."

"No," he said fiercely. "Jody would never do this to me."

"Wouldn't she?"

"She cared for me."

"She did."

"She would understand."

"Would she?"

"Yes. Yes. No matter what I did. She would forgive."

"Forgive?"

"Yes."

"Fool."

"This is a trick," he shouted. "Someone's playing a trick on me."

"Fool, all life is a trick."

The voice laughed harshly.

"Stop it," he pleaded.

"I'll never stop it."

"I can't stand it anymore."

"I know."

"You'll drive me to suicide. I'll kill myself."

"Exactly."

He didn't say anything. His face was white and taut in the shadows.

"Then I will rest. And you will rest. If you can."

The phone clicked.

He stood there and began to moan.

But there was no one in the house to hear him.

No one.

Chapter
36

He sat on the empty beach gazing out to the horizon. The day was ending—the long, bleak day—and now the sun was beginning to fall into the sea.

Soon it will be night, he thought. Dark and starless night.

It has to be this way.

On this night of all nights there will be no stars, no moon, only desolate darkness.

This night of all nights.

As soon as it comes I shall walk out into the water and then begin my swim, my last and final one.

I shall swim, far, far out, as Jody did, swim until I can go on no more, and then I will slowly and surely sink deep into the water and find my rest.

If I can.

He heard his name called.

"Paul."

He slowly turned and saw the figure come over to him, the twilight falling over its face and body.

It was Joe Carson.

He stood there looking down at Paul.

"Hello, Paul."

"Hello, Joe," Paul said in a toneless voice.

"I was walking the beach and I saw you."

The man stood there, his face impassive. "I just got back from Florida."

"Oh."

"I'm here for a few days," Joe said.

Paul was silent.

"How are things with you?"

"All right."

The man's eyes scanned him.

"You don't look all right to me."

Paul didn't speak.

"Mind if I sit down?"

"No."

Carson sat down near him and looked out to the sea. The last faint rays of the sun played over the water, staining it a soft bronze.

And Paul thought of Jody's golden hair and her white flashing hand waving in the dying sunlight, waving to him to come out and join her.

His eyes glowed for an instant.

"We both love the sea, don't we?" Carson said in a low voice.

"I guess so."

"Ever since I was a child. The same with you, isn't it?"

"Yes," Paul murmured.

Carson turned to him, waited, and then spoke.

"I've thought a lot about you, Paul. While I was down in Boca."

"Did you?"

The man nodded. "An awful lot. You gave me no peace."

The darkness will soon come in, Paul thought.

And nothing will matter anymore.

"I judged you too severely," Carson said.

It doesn't matter anymore, Joe.

"And now I'm sure of that. Particularly after I had a talk with your friend, Joan Bradley."

Paul turned to him.

"Joan?"

"Yes. She came to see me this afternoon."

"And?"

"She told me how much you were suffering over what happened."

"She say anything else?"

The man shook his head. "Just that you were very close to a breakdown. She wanted me to speak to you. Pleaded with me."

"Joan?"

"She cares very much for you, Paul."

Paul's hands clenched and then unclenched.

"Paul, I've been looking all over for you. You're on my conscience, son."

Paul turned away from him and didn't speak.

"I was very bitter with you. Over what you did," Joe said.

"You had a right to be," Paul murmured.

"Maybe I did. But I shouldn't have made out the harsh report I did on you. The same one I sent to Jody Miller's sister."

"What?"

"She wanted you put in prison. At least I stopped that."

"Jody had a sister?"

"Yes. Didn't you know that?"

Paul shook his head silently.

"That's all she had left. A sister."

"She knows what happened?"

"Yes."

Paul looked out to the darkening sea and felt like weeping.

Finally he was able to speak.

"Did you ever see her?"

"No."

"Speak to her?"

"Only by phone."

"She hates me, doesn't she?"

Carson didn't answer him.

"Hates me with her soul. She's almost out of her mind with hatred for me. Isn't that so, Joe?"

The man stared at Paul and then silently nodded.

Paul looked away from him and out to the sea. Then his eyes moved inward to the breakers, crashing their snowy foam onto the dim beach.

Cold, white, and chilling foam.

He turned back to Carson, his face taut.

"Joe, listen to me. Please. You saw Jody a few times."

"Yes."

"You heard her speak. Enough to know her voice."

"It was a voice that is hard to forget," Joe said.

"It is."

"Well?"

Paul hesitated and then spoke.

"Was her sister's voice like Jody's?"

"Yes."

"Very much like it?"

"I would say about the same."

"The same?"

Carson nodded.

"Yes. I remember having the uncanny feeling that I was talking to Jody Miller."

Paul trembled.

Carson leaned over to him and put his hand on Paul's shoulder.

"Are you all right?"

"It can't be possible," Paul said.

"What, Paul?"

"It can't be."

He slowly rose to his feet.

"Thanks, Joe," he murmured.

And then he walked away from the man and into the oncoming darkness.

Chapter
37

And now the night had come down, dark and starless, enveloping him.

He stood alone on the sand and listened to the relentless waves sweeping in to shore.

Calling him into the water.

Ever calling.

But beneath their cry, he heard another voice.

Jody had a sister.

A sister.

Sister.

Suddenly he turned and left the beach and the sound of the ocean.

Chapter
38

He was lying in bed, looking up at the ceiling, dimly white in the night darkness, when he heard the sound of bits of gravel being thrown against the window of his room.

He got out of bed and went to the window and looked down into the garden, and there she was, standing between two gaunt trees.

Her voice floated up to him in a whisper, yet he heard every word.

"You haven't killed yourself yet?"

"No."

"But you will."

"No. You're not Jody."

"I'm not."

"You're her sister."

And he thought he could see her flinch.

But he could not be sure.

"Oh?"

There was a faint, cruel smile in her eyes.

"Joe Carson told me."

"Did he?"

"He spoke to you."

"I see."

She leaned against one of the trees, her face white, and he could see the glint of moonlight on her golden hair.

"You're not Jody."

"I'm her twin sister."

"Yes."

"Jody had no sisters. Jody is alone in this cold, cold world."

He stood there looking down at her.

"Alone and dead, dear Paul. Dead."

A soft breeze came up and fluttered the small leaves of the trees. And he thought he could hear the faint, silvery sound of little bells.

The breeze faded, but the sound of the bells lingered.

Soft, ever so soft.

He put his hands to his ears to shut out the sound.

But as he did, he heard her say, in an icy whisper, "Paul, Joe Carson hates you as much as I do. He's lying to you."

"No," Paul murmured.

"Yes. He wanted you in prison. I want you dead. That is our only difference. We hate you equally."

She began to laugh that low, harsh laugh that chilled his blood.

"You're close," she said. "So very close. A little push and you'll be over the brink."

He shivered.

"Just a little push."

Then he saw her move back into the darkness, and he could see her no more.

Chapter
39

He broke into the storage shed and then lugged one of the lifeguard stands out onto the sand.

He looked around him and all was silence.

The sun was still high in a bright and cloudless sky, but there was no one else on the wide swathe of beach.

Only the gray gulls with their glittering eyes.

Then he took a deep breath, bent over, and began dragging the heavy stand over the white sand, cutting two deep tracks into it.

He had to pause every few minutes to rest, his chest heaving and the muscles of his big arms tight.

The sweat gleamed on his arms, his legs, and his bare chest.

He wore his white pith helmet.

His large striped towel lay over one of the steps of the stand.

It took him a full half-hour to come to the spot.

When he reached it, he rested for a few minutes, and then he called upon every ounce of his great strength and pulled the stand into an upright position.

He took off the white pith helmet and stood there, looking up at the high stand.

The seat at its top caught the sun and glowed.

This is where I used to sit, he thought.

Like a king.

King of my wide and serene domain.

This is where it all started.

And this is where it will end.

There was a wild look in his hazel eyes.

She will come here.

She will.

She knows every move I make.

She will come.

I'm sure of it.

For she is as mad as I am.

One push and I'll be over the brink, she said.

I think I'm over it already.

Paul slowly climbed up to the top and then sat down.

He put on his white pith helmet.

And then his dark glasses.

He draped the striped towel over his shoulders.

And waited.

Waited for Jody to come to him.

Or would it be her sister?

Chapter

40

The night was full with stars, and the moon was bright and shining, spreading its silver light over the empty beach.

Empty and still.

The waves of the sea glimmered.

He sat on the stand.

Still waiting.

Never doubting that she would come.

Then the sea became quiet. Quiet and expectant. As he listened to its gentle and constant murmur, his senses began to dull and soon his eyes began to close.

His head dropped.

The pith helmet slid off his head and dropped with a soft thud onto the sand below.

His hands fell limply to his sides.

Now his eyes closed shut.

The moon moved behind a drift of clouds and the sky darkened.

The beach was completely silent.

It was then that he heard the voice.

"Paul."

He heard it again.

"Paul."

He slowly opened his eyes.

"I'm here," the voice said.

He looked and there she was, standing by the shore, on the very lip of the shore, as if she had just come out of the dark and murmuring sea.

She wore the silk blouse and the slacks, and her hair, her golden hair, was swept back into a bun.

Her white purse was slung over her shoulder.

"Take off your glasses so I can see your eyes," she said gently.

"Jody?"

"No."

"Then who are you?"

"You know that now, Paul."

"Her sister?"

"Yes."

She moved closer to the stand.

"We were born on the same day, the same hour."

Her voice was low in the vast night.

"We died on the same day, the same hour."

He looked away from her burning eyes and into the darkness.

Then he heard her voice again, and this time it was closer to him.

"When you killed Jody, you killed me, too."

"Why do you tell me this now?"

"Because after tonight you will never see me again."

He turned to her and now she was on the dry sand, just below him, and he could see her clearly.

She had never come that close to him before.

Now he saw the tiny scar on her cheek.

Tiny but distinct.

"I have a scar," she said. "Just as you have on your chin."

His hand went impulsively to his tiny scar and then dropped away.

"Jody told me everything about you. Everything. How

much she loved you. And I came to love you just as much as she did."

Her eyes looked desperately up into his.

"Even more, Paul."

"Even more," he whispered.

"Yes."

Then he heard her voice again.

"Why did you kill us, Paul? Why?"

The moon came from behind the clouds, and now he could see her white, shining hand go to her purse and slowly open it.

"She was so beautiful. You destroyed such beauty. She had such immense talent. Talent I never had. I lived through her, Paul. She would have become one of the greatest of all ballet dancers. Everybody waited for her to become that. The world. And you destroyed it all. All, Paul."

She began to weep silently.

He bowed his head.

"You drove me mad with hatred for you. I wanted to torture you just as you tortured me. And in the end. . . ."

He heard her voice no more.

Only the soft sound of the waves.

He raised his head and saw her take a gun from her purse.

"I've come to kill you, Paul."

He nodded silently.

"I know," he said.

She pointed the gun up at him.

Her sea green eyes flashed.

"If killing me will bring you rest—then do it," he said.

She didn't speak.

She still held the gun pointed up at him.

He shook his head sadly.

"But it won't. Can't you see that? There is no rest for you. No rest for me. That's how it is. We're the haunted ones."

He saw the gun waver.

"The haunted ones," he said again, his voice breaking.

135

Then he came slowly down from the stand and stood close to her.

"But we have to go on. And there's nothing we can do about it. Just go on and try to live our lives out as best we can. We have to."

He reached out and took the gun from her. Then he turned and flung it far out where it caught the sheen of the moon and then sank rapidly and was gone into the water.

He reached his hand out to her and touched her shoulder.

She trembled and he saw how much she still loved him.

Still.

He held her close and it was the same as holding Jody, and he closed his eyes with the sweet pain, and when he opened them again she was gone out of his arms and he stood there.

Watching her slowly disappear.

Into the waning night.

About the Author

Jay Bennett, a master of suspense, was the first writer to win in two successive years the Mystery Writers of America's prestigious Edgar Allen Poe Award for Best Juvenile Mystery. His last book, *The Skeleton Man*, was nominated for the 1986 Edgar Allen Poe Award. He is the author of many suspense novels for young adults as well as successful adult novels, stage plays, and television scripts. Mr. Bennett lives in Cherry Hill, New Jersey.

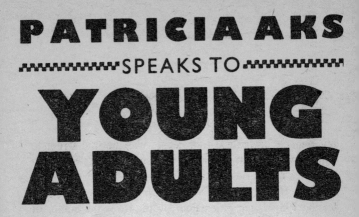